Ethelred
Preston

OR THE ADVENTURES
OF A NEWCOMER

"Your money or your life!"

Ethelred Preston

OR THE ADVENTURES OF A NEWCOMER

By

Fr. Francis J. Finn, S.J.
AUTHOR OF TOM PLAYFAIR, PERCY WYNN,
HARRY DEE, ETC.

TAN BOOKS AND PUBLISHERS, INC.
Rockford, Illinois 61105

Published in approximately 1897 by Benziger Brothers, New York.

Retypeset and published in 2003 by TAN Books and Publishers, Inc.

ISBN 0-89555-714-2

Library of Congress Control No.: 2001-132400

Cover illustration © 2002 by Phyllis Pollema-Cahill. Cover illustration expressly rendered for this book and used by arrangement with Wilkinson Studios, Chicago.

Cover design by Peter Massari, Rockford, Illinois.

Printed and bound in the United States of America.

TAN BOOKS AND PUBLISHERS, INC.
P.O. Box 424
Rockford, Illinois 61105

2003

"Father Edmunds was a man whom long experience as a disciplinarian and as a superior had schooled in the control of his emotions. But as he entered the parlor and glanced at the new pupil he started back, while a slight exclamation forced itself from his lips. And he had reason for being astonished." —Page 9

CONTENTS

Ethelred Preston

OR THE ADVENTURES OF A NEWCOMER

Chapter I

A LETTER FROM ETHELRED'S MAMA

SEATED at his desk on a bright Wednesday morning toward the end of January, Father Edmunds, the reverend president of Henryton College, was gazing with a look of weariness upon the enormous mass of papers, pamphlets and letters piled up before him. The gaze and the weariness lasted but a moment; then he fixed his eyeglasses firmly upon his nose and set to work at distributing. While slipping the letters from his hand to a table at his side, he scanned their superscriptions, dropping some to the right and a great many to his left. The larger pile thus formed was made up of letters addressed to the students; the smaller, of those addressed to himself and his community. From the letters Father Edmunds went to the pamphlets, magazines and newspapers; and here the wastebasket came into service. With a dexterity born of long experience, the president could ascertain, in most cases at a glance, and without opening their wrappers, the general

1

character of the enclosed missives. Before he had done with examining these, the waste-basket had received a very generous moiety of current literature. The morning's mail thus sorted, Father Edmunds touched his bell, in answer to which a young gentleman, his private secretary, entered the room.

"For the vice president," said Father Edmunds, pointing to the mail of the students.

The secretary bowed, took the mail in his hands and withdrew.

Having thus narrowed his field of labor, Father Edmunds addressed himself to a more careful examination. Again taking up the letters, he selected his own. Opening these, he skimmed rapidly over the first five, pigeon-holing three and dropping two into the waste-basket. But the sixth letter gave him pause.

It was enclosed in a dainty, scented, square envelope, and was a very lengthy production. Setting aside the evidence of the perfumery, the communication was evidently the work of a woman; it was written down and across the page in fat sprawling letters, where m's and w's and x's and v's were utterly indistinguishable. Father Edmunds sighed; he had struggled through such letters before. Nothing could be skipped, nothing taken for granted. Not infrequently the most important part of such missives was to be found where crossings were thickest. He began, then, the reading with mild resignation. Suddenly an expression of awakening interest came upon his features. As he reached the third page a smile began to flicker; it burst into a flame at the fourth, and blazed on merrily to the end, when he exclaimed:

"Little Lord Fauntleroy the second!"

He laughed quietly, and added:

"I fancy the small boys of Henryton College are going to be awakened from their mid-winter dullness. I must see the vice president at once."

"Father Howard," he exclaimed, as he entered the vice president's room a moment later, "have you room in the junior division for a Little Lord Fauntleroy?"

"I have, certainly; but I'm not so sure about the boys. They may try, in their innocent but abrupt way, to find out whether he is really and truly real."

"Well, it would appear that he is real enough; just read this letter."

Father Howard took the scented envelope, drew out the enclosure—and this is what he read:

Reverend Edmund C. Edmunds

Reverend Dear Sir: It is after reflection and thought and many tears that I address myself to your kindness. I now find myself, dear reverend sir, forced to face a trial, which, alas, but one week ago I could not so much as have fancied. My darling little boy and I must part. Ah, dear Father, if you but knew what that meant. No one but a mother can appreciate the grief which fills my heart. The dear child is the picture of his father. He is lovely and innocent and has never been away from my side—not even for one day. Whatever he knows—and he has gone quite far in spelling and botany, including the language of flowers—I have taught him myself, and in my teachings I have addressed myself to the heart rather than to the head. He is not at all like other boys, of whom it may be said that they are uniformly rude, but has all the refinements of a young lady. He is docile, amiable, cheerful, happy as the day is long—the sweetest child imaginable. All his little ways are lovely. He is generous to a fault, in which he resembles his father, and is as sensitive as I was in the days of my youth, and conscientious to a degree approaching scrupulosity. And yet I am not, after the fashion of most mothers, blind to his faults. My little Ethelred is just the least trifle impetuous and inconsiderate. By those who do not understand him, he might even be called thoughtless. Nevertheless, he is *so* open to reason! A little talk, if kindly and considerately given and accompanied with a little coaxing, will never fail to bring him to his senses. He has never been subjected to corporal punishment—the dear child is high-strung, and *so* nervous, and would be injured for life by such barbarous treatment. *Under no circumstance must this child be touched—* this point I insist upon.

Ethelred is a delicate child. Just after teething he contracted a severe illness. [Here the fond mother goes into a detailed account of all Master Ethelred's various ailments and maladies, mentioning incidentally, but at some length, several diseases which, by an especial providence, he had just narrowly escaped. As these details are of little interest to the public at large, and do not bear directly upon the story, I omit them.]

Now, dear reverend sir, in view of what I have told you, you must see how necessary it is that the greatest care be taken of Ethelred's health. He should get a glass of milk at least four times a day— twice in the morning and twice in the afternoon.

"The boy should by all means bring a cow along," muttered the vice president.

> If possible, he should have sweet bread every morning at breakfast, a glass of port wine at dinner, and dry toast at supper.

"He should bring his cook along too," interjected the president.

> Ethelred is not a Catholic. I am an Episcopalian in theory, and my dear boy will probably join the same church. I am not a bigoted woman, and believe that there are good Catholics, many of whom will doubtless go to Heaven. My boy is naturally very religious, and I send him to your school because I understand that the moral training there is excellent. Miss Martin, whose nephew, Earl Meriwether, attends your College, gives me an excellent account of it. I do not know Earl personally, though his lamented mother and I were most *intimate* friends at school, and I feel that Earl, whose reputation stands very high, will be a suitable companion for my boy—as far as *any boy* can be a suitable companion for one who has had such home training as my Ethelred has enjoyed. If there are any *good* Catholic boys attending your College, supposing, of course, that their manners make some such approach toward refinement as we have reason to expect of

boys of the better class, I see no objection to my boy's associating with them *under due inspection.*

I am so agitated, dear reverend sir, that I find it almost impossible to put my thoughts on paper with any appearance of order. I should 'ere this have explained to you my reason for being obliged to separate myself from my sweet child. It is inevitable. Yesterday I received a telegram from London, England, stating that my husband has there been attacked by hemorrhages, and that his position is precarious.

Of course I must start by the next steamer. Gladly would I bring my little Ethelred along, but the poor child is so sensitive to seasickness that it would be literally flying in the face of providence to imperil his precious health—mayhap his life—by taking him along. The parting is difficult, but it must be made. Again and again I beg you to bestow every attention upon my darling, and *a mother's prayer* and *a mother's blessing* will accompany you through life.

Thanking you in advance for your kindness, and asking you to overlook the inaccuracies and blunders of a well-nigh distracted mother, I am, dear reverend sir, Yours most earnestly and beseechingly,

ELEANOR PRESTON

P.S. Enclosed you will find a check or a draught or a bank note (I am not quite sure of the correct term) for four hundred dollars for Ethelred's expenses. On reaching London I shall forward more. My child will reach you on Thursday morning. I have been holding him back in hopes of getting some trusted friend to accompany him on his trip. I would go myself, but could hardly do so without missing the first steamer. Be a father, dear reverend sir, to my precious darling.

E. P.

"Such a boy," the president remarked, "hardly requires testimonials as to his character."

"Not if he's anything at all like what his mother makes him out to be," answered Father Howard. "Let us hope that he really is a swan in the eyes of others than his fond parent. Meantime it would be good to write for references. If you have no objection, I shall attend to that part of the matter myself."

And there was no objection.

On the next morning, at about the same hour, the college porter brought Father Edmunds a card. He read with a smile—

Master Ethelred Preston,
Albany Villa, Brighton
[At Home Tuesdays]

"I'm on my road to meet our Little Lord Fauntleroy," said Father Edmunds as he encountered the vice president in the hall.

Father Edmunds was a man whom long experience as a disciplinarian and as a superior had schooled in the control of his emotions. But as he entered the parlor and glanced at the new pupil he started back, while a slight exclamation forced itself from his lips. And he had reason for being astonished.

Chapter II

IN WHICH THINGS BEGIN TO GO BADLY WITH EARL MERIWETHER

WHILE Father Edmunds was mastering his astonishment in the parlor, matters were not proceeding with their wonted smoothness in the class of First Academic.

There was a frown upon the brow of the professor, Mr. Gade. He was explaining the sequence of tenses (for the fortieth or fiftieth time, be it said) and eyeing, as he spoke, a young gentleman in one of the corner seats. If he counted upon catching the pupil's eye he must have been disappointed. The boy was scribbling very industriously and, according to all seeming, utterly oblivious of everything about him, save the sheet of paper across which his pencil was travelling.

The professor finally paused; his face turned a shade paler, and the ominous frown deepened upon his forehead. Everyone in the class with the exception of the scribbler showed manifest signs of uneasiness.

"This thing has gone too far!" said Mr. Gade, changing his tone of voice. He spoke low because he was indignant. At the words, Earl Meriwether, the scribbler, looked up inquiringly.

"Yes, Meriwether, I mean *you*. For five minutes I have been explaining the sequence of tenses, principally for your benefit. The theme you handed in this morning shows me that if you ever knew anything about the construction of a Latin sentence, you have almost utterly forgotten it. And now, while I explain, you must devote yourself to other work. I have been very much disappointed in you of late. Your conduct has pained and annoyed me. Please leave the room."

Mr. Gade seldom spoke in reproof to his pupils; but when he did so speak, his admonitions carried weight. The boys valued his kind words and, loving him, dreaded his displeasure above all punishment. There had fallen a strained silence upon the room as the professor spoke, and one could see by the expressions on the students' faces that the scene was painful and unusual. Meriwether himself had first given a start when his name was called out, and as Mr. Gade had gone on, a look of pained surprise had come upon his features. At the command to leave the room he turned very red, compressed his lips and, putting his hands into his pockets, strode out with something of a swagger. This air of defiance in the manner of his exit confirmed Mr. Gade in the impression that the rebuke was well merited.

Then the classwork proceeded as usual, and yet with a difference. The boys were serious and subdued in manner, and the little undercurrent of pleasantry, which often exists in a class along with perfect order and attention, and which certain professors of sunny temperament find it to their account to foster, was congealed for that day.

"It was like the funeral without the carriage ride," said Roger Haines to Edward Devereux as they came out together into the playground at recess.

"So it was," assented Devereux. "A fellow doesn't know how much fun he's having in our class till something goes wrong; and then we know it by not having it. But what's coming over Earl Meriwether anyhow these last few weeks? He used to be a great friend of Mr. Gade's, and never handed in a single paper that wasn't among the very best. Yesterday when Mr. Gade passed a lot of us fellows in the yard we all took off our hats to him except Earl. And the worst of it was that Earl walked right past Mr. Gade and took no notice at all of his nod and smile. Our teacher flushed, and we could see that he was annoyed. Something has gone wrong with Earl. He doesn't seem to be the same boy at all that he used to be. He never was very lively; but now he's positively gloomy. He's the best friend I ever had, and it makes me blue to see him going down in this way. I am really puzzled about the whole thing. He's the most popular boy in the school still, but he's going to lose his popularity if he doesn't take care."

"I thought there would be a row soon," said Roger. "Earl has got to be very negligent in his studies, and from being the leader he is now getting down to the foot. I don't think he has given a good recitation for the last two or three weeks, and I've been expecting Mr. Gade to call him down this long time."

"I feel very bad about the whole affair," continued Devereux. "Earl and I have been chums, and besides liking him, I respect him more than any boy I ever met. Of late he hasn't been with me. He's always in the reading-room and doesn't do anything but read and take notes. I have felt like having a good talk with him a dozen times, but the chance has never offered itself, and I have been too careless to put myself to a little trouble."

"You ought to talk to Earl, Ed. If you don't, I'll do it myself, though I don't know him near as well as you do."

"All right, I'll do it, though I'm afraid that he will hardly be in any humor just now for anything I have to say."

"There he is over near the playroom; catch him, and strike while the iron is hot."

"I say, Earl," said Devereux a moment

later, as he placed his hand on Earl's shoulder and fell into step with him on the walk running beside the playroom, "what's the trouble between you and Mr. Gade? You used to get along so well with him, and now it's all at sixes and sevens between you."

Ed paused for an answer, but none came. He looked up presently into Earl's face, and then he understood. Earl's face was quivering with emotion, and there was a suspicious moisture in his eyes.

"Oh, I say, Earl, don't take it so hard," pleaded soft-hearted Ed. "We all get a scolding now and then, you know, and I suppose that most of us deserve it every time."

"Do you think I deserved that scolding?" asked Earl.

"Since you ask it," returned Ed, "I must say I do. All the fellows think the same."

Again Earl's features were convulsed; he struggled for a moment, and then, unable longer to restrain himself, he broke away from his astonished and dismayed companion and, seeking a retired spot, gave full vent to his emotion. This was Earl's third year at College, and Ed Devereux was the first and only boy who had ever seen him shed a tear.

The few minutes of the present recess

promised to be of importance in the shaping of Earl's life. Matters had seemingly come to a head. Earl had been a student at Henryton College for two years and a half. During this period he had enjoyed the popularity of the boys and the respect of the faculty. He was a lad of a somewhat serious turn of mind, remarkably earnest in everything, and very noticeable for his piety. He was a Lutheran, and practiced his religion in a manner that surprised and edified his fellow students. Indeed his simple and frank piety had often put to shame some of the more negligent Catholic boys. His conduct in the chapel and at prayers was such that many of his companions had been as long as a year with him before learning that he was not of their religion.

He won the name of being a deeply religious lad early in his first year at Henryton. It happened during the celebration of the Holy Sacrifice of the Mass, at which, according to the custom of Henryton College, all the students assisted. The boy next him was behaving rather lightly and several times tried to secure Earl's attention. Earl, with his eyes fastened upon his own book of devotion, refused to recognize his companion's advances. After Mass, however, he awaited the irreverent youngster outside.

"Ed Devereux, I'm going to ask you an honest question, and I want an honest answer. Will you give it?"

"Why of course," returned Ed.

"Do you really believe that Christ is present in the Blessed Sacrament of the Altar?"

"If I were able, I'd lick the man who said I didn't," returned tiny Ed, with flashing eyes and considerable vehemence.

"Well, then, I can't for the life of me understand how you can carry on in the chapel the way you do, if you really believe. I'm not a Catholic myself, and I certainly never will be one; but I try to show reverence in chapel out of respect for the opinions of the Catholic boys around me. I don't understand your position, Ed."

When Ed learned then and there for the first time that the boy who sat beside him at services was not a Catholic, he started with dismay and surprise, and the rebuke humbled him as he never had been humbled before. His face flushed scarlet. He looked in dumb, pitiful distress at Earl for a moment and then returned to the chapel. From that hour dated Ed Devereux's profound reverence for the Real Presence; from that hour dated his love and respect for Earl

Meriwether, which had gone on increasing month by month.

He did not answer Earl's question, and indeed never referred to that conversation but once. Then he said:

"Earl, when you spoke to me about my behavior in the chapel, you said among other things that you never intended to become a Catholic. Did you really mean that?"

"Indeed I did," answered Earl.

"Well, I hope that my disgraceful conduct had nothing to do with your intention. It's been bothering me ever since."

"That had nothing whatever to do with my resolve," said Earl.

"Well, perhaps my conduct along with the conduct of some of the other fellows may have been the cause. Now you know, Earl, we all of us Catholic boys here believe all right—but we are young and giddy, I suppose, and don't think. Some of us trifle at times in the chapel, without thinking of what we are doing. Sometimes a boy actually doesn't know that he is fooling. There's a boy here now who seems to be most irreverent in the chapel, and yet I know that he prays hard, and all the fellows know that he wouldn't do anything wrong for the world. Yet, if you watch him at services, you would hardly think him a Catholic. You see—"

"Hold on!" cried Earl, "you needn't explain the way some of you fellows carry on: I wouldn't understand any explanation anyhow. It wasn't on that account either that I made my resolve. The fact is, I made a promise that I would be true to my own religion when I was a little boy of seven, nearly eight years ago."

"You did?"

"Yes; would you like to hear how it happened?"

"Indeed I would."

"It's a long story, Ed, and you're the only person I've ever offered to tell it to."

Devereux's face flushed with genuine pleasure at these words. He had come to look up to this Lutheran boy with an admiration which was made up of reverence and love. Such a friendship is rarely inspired. It supposes on the part of him who is thus admired a strength of character, a sincerity and a manliness that are seldom found in one person.

"Nothing would please me better than to hear it," said Ed.

"It's a long story, as I said, and not particularly interesting in itself. I wouldn't think even of telling it to you, only I know and value the interest you take in me, and feel sure that you will be interested."

And with this somewhat awkward introduction, Earl told his story.

Now as Earl's early life has much to do with what is to come, I shall tell the reader Meriwether's history as he related it to Ed, with certain details such as the honest boy's modesty forbade him divulge even to his bosom friend.

Chapter III

THE STORY OF EARL

EARL Meriwether was the son of a Catholic father and a Protestant mother. At least that was what the world said. As a matter of fact, his father was hardly a Catholic, even in the loosest and most strained sense of the word. Mr. Meriwether had been baptized in a Catholic church, which was the beginning of his Catholicity—and the end. Trained in a sectarian school, he had contented himself with asserting that he was a Catholic because his parents were of that faith. In practice he was of no religion. Three years after leaving school, he married an accomplished and devout young lady, and Earl was their only child. It was shortly after Earl's birth that Mr. Meriwether fell into habits of dissipation. Between him and his passions there stood no bar of restraint in the shape of religion. To Earl's mother, Mr. Meriwether was the embodiment of Catholic teaching and practice. She was shocked by his evil courses and attributed them to the religion which he had never attempted to practice. The gentle lady was horrified at the wild excesses of her husband. By their fruits you shall know them, she argued; and, in consequence, the Catholic Church became to her a name of horror and reproach.

Brooding day after day over the wreckage of a life to which, for better or for worse, she had irrevocably bound her own, she fell into a decline. The end came very soon. Little Earl was with her through all these dark days, and from the first faint dawn of reason gave an attentive ear to his mother's pious teachings and counsels. Upon the child her tender devotion and deep religious spirit created a lasting impression, and his young heart was attuned from the first to exalted standards of goodness, such as only a tender and pious mother can awaken. Insensibly, too, the boy caught something of the austere gravity of his mother. He had little of what is called light-heartedness. There was a seriousness about him which accompanied him even in his sports and amusements. He seldom laughed.

Then there came a day when he was summoned to the bedside of his mother for the last time. She held him long to her bosom, and after the first passionate, almost incoherent greeting of love, she recovered herself and, in terms that had been carefully weighed and studied, laid upon him her last injunctions in regard to his spiritual welfare.

"And now, my child," she said finally, "I ask you to give me your solemn word that you will be true to your religion—true till we meet again in a brighter world."

With his arms about his mother's neck, the boy sobbed out the words of promise; and they came from his heart.

No more was said. There was a last, tender embrace, and then he was taken from the room. When he was brought back some hours later, the tender hand that had pressed his so recently lay still upon the coverlid; and the mild, sweet eyes that had beamed love were closed forever, while upon the gentle features lay the peace of God.

In accordance with his mother's desire, Earl was placed in the care of her younger sister. His father, broken by excesses, shortly followed her to the grave. Strangely enough, the younger sister—within the year of Mrs. Meriwether's death—became a convert to the Catholic Faith. However, she made no endeavors to interfere with Earl's religion, but encouraged him in the pious practices which his mother had taught him.

At the age of twelve, Earl was sent to Henryton College, and from his entrance, as has already been said, he proved himself to be a thoroughly good boy. A leader in the class, a leader in the yard, up to the time of the opening of the present story, Earl's record was untarnished. Then his troubles had begun. It was evident to everyone that he was no longer the close and conscientious student that he once had been. In class his attention flagged; upon the campus he no longer took a leading part in the sports and games. In a word, a decided and most disappointing change had come to pass. Mr. Gade was much concerned. To him, his class was everything; no wonder, then, that the conduct of Earl had wounded him deeply. He had intended calling the boy to account privately, and was only awaiting a favorable opportunity, when Earl's inattention in class precipitated matters. The scolding thus given publicly had been received in such a way that Mr. Gade was deeply mortified. His hold upon Earl, thought the professor, was lost forever. Earl had gone beyond the reach of his influence. The boy, he reasoned, had deliberately thrown off the restraints of discipline and chosen a downward path. Earl, to all seeming, had made no attempt for the past three weeks to conceal his growing dislike of studies. The frankness which had characterized him in his intercourse with his teacher had been replaced by a coldness and reserve which could be interpreted in only one light.

Mr. Gade, although of a highly nervous disposition, was a man of more than ordinary prudence and tact. In dealing with his young charges, he rarely made mistakes of judgment, and in the present case, accordingly, he had no suspicion that he might possibly be wrong. And yet he was in the wrong. Without fault on his part, he had misunderstood Earl throughout.

A few weeks before the opening of this story, the college students had made, as was their yearly custom, a retreat of three days. The exercises were given by a widely known missionary priest, a man who could thrill, by his eloquence in the pulpit, even those familiar friends who in the common inter-course of life recognized in him as his salient traits a marvellous simplicity and lowliness. Earl, partly through a craving for the light and consolation of religion, partly through the desire of hearing a man famed for his burning eloquence, attended the various instructions and, from the first words that fell from the good Father's lips, was rapt and fascinated. Earl, at that period, had reached the stage of physical development when the human passions are wont to awake to a dangerous activity and arise in all their strength. Thus far, the sweet and untainted stream of his innocent life had run on its way smooth and uncheckered. But now, and with sudden transition, the running was through devious and perilous ways. Earl was frightened. He dreaded sin as few boys dread it; and yet, do what he might, he saw daily, sometimes hourly, its face, not foul and hideous as he knew it to be in reality, but tricked out with the specious beauties and masked under the enticing allurements which it knows so well how to assume. Sometimes in the solemn watches of the night, sometimes in the hours devoted to study, now in the intervals between play and class, now in the classroom itself—that face of sin with its poisonous beauty hovered about him and before him, and despite his resistance still hovered, still came nearer and nearer.

The day that preceded the beginning of the retreat was the most troubled of his life. It was a day out of which he came free from serious sin, but bruised and bleeding, nevertheless, from a long, bitter fight with temptation. He went to bed weary and despondent. Though a conqueror—poor boy!—in the silence of the dormitory there seemed to sound in his heart a voice: "You cannot keep it up! Think of it! It will be the same fight day after day, hour after hour—with this difference—that, as you grow older, your passions and temptations shall wax stronger. It is impossible for you to keep on."

It was the voice of the tempter—the lying voice which perverts truth in every possible way. It was the voice of him who, when he cannot conquer the strong soul by direct attack, strives to weaken it by discouragement. Next to virtue, the devil hates cheerfulness.

And Earl tried to turn his ear from that voice—for he suspected the source from which it came—and thus trying, slept. He fell asleep, feeling very miserable and unhappy. In that place where things are seen, not as they appear, but as they really are, I doubt not that this unhappy day of Earl's was regarded as full of beauty and sovereign merit; and, if his Guardian Angel could have but communicated what he knew to the sleeping boy, Earl's face, dejected and troubled even in sleep, would have grown radiant with joy.

When on the following day he heard the Reverend Father depict, with the vividness of the practiced and eloquent missioner, the hideousness of sin, and describe the methods of fighting against it; when, above all, he warned his young hearers against sadness, and roused them to confidence, hope and cheerfulness—Earl was carried away with enthusiasm. Every word from the Father's lips seemed to be directed to himself; every word struck home. At the close of the retreat he obtained a personal interview with the Father, from which he came away at once strengthened and troubled: strengthened, for he was resolved to fight bravely, to hope confidently; troubled, for he felt bound, on the one hand, to keep true to the promise which he had made his mother and, on the other, bound to inquire more closely into the doctrine and discipline of the Catholic Church, which approved itself to his mind and heart as being the true Church of Christ.

Thus the retreat, while drawing Earl away, for the time being, from the slippery brink of sin, had plunged him into a phase of doubt and distress, all the more painful that, through a natural reticence, he could not bring himself to consult or advise with anyone.

Absorbed, then, in these mental trials, he had found it exceedingly difficult to fix his attention upon the daily affairs of life, and almost impossible to give his mind for any length of time to his studies. In consequence, his position in class changed rapidly; and he who had in other years been the promptest to answer, the quickest to learn, was now inattentive, restless and, at times, almost stupid.

At last came the day when he received, for the first time since his coming to college, a public rebuke in the classroom. He had been struggling hard on that eventful morning to pay attention and, although he was scribbling mechanically at the moment of rebuke, he had not missed a single word of Mr. Gade's explanation. There are some students whose attention is at the highest point when they are apparently engrossed with something else. Earl, at this troublous period, belonged to this class.

When Mr. Gade, fastening his eyes on Earl said, "Yes, Meriwether; I mean you," the boy was shocked. The rebuke was so unexpected, and, as Earl saw the matter, so undeserved, that he left the room with a bitter sense of outraged justice.

Boys are like men. They are prone to identify a principle with its exponent, to judge of the truth or falsity of a religion by their likes or dislikes for those representatives of the creed with whom they come in closest contact.

"That settles it!" muttered Earl as, quivering with rage, he paced up and down the deserted playground: "I'll never be a Catholic as long as I live! I'll show Mr. Gade that he can't walk over me as he pleases."

And he fell into a train of ugly resolutions, the wretched outcome of wounded vanity and mortified pride.

Earl, be it remembered, was a good boy; but even good boys have the passions of their kind. Earl was a reasonable, fair-minded boy, too; but even reasonable, fair-minded people are sometimes carried away by their feelings. His resolution never to become a Catholic was, in view of the circumstances, illogical and petulant; but it was a strong resolution for all that.

These interior struggles and feelings Earl did not tell to Eddie Devereux. He gave many of the facts set down in this chapter, but omitted or unintentionally misinterpreted the underlying motives. Eddie, in consequence, though he now comprehended his friend's position better, was by no means able to understand the exact state of the question. After receiving the kind sympathy of his best friend, Earl was returning to the classroom, still sore and angry, still determined to show by his manner how aggrieved he was, when Father Howard beckoned him aside.

"Earl, there's a friend of yours in the parlor."

"Who is it, Father?"

"Did you ever hear of Ethelred Preston?"

"Yes, sir; is he here? I never saw him, but I met his mother once. She and my mother were school girls together and were very intimate. She seemed to be a very refined lady, and she did nothing but talk about Ethelred all the time. I suppose he's a sort of a wax doll, isn't he?"

"He's his mama's darling!" And when Father Howard had said this, he turned his face away so as to conceal a smile. "Go to the parlor, Earl. You must try to take care of dainty little Ethelred till he feels perfectly at home."

Then Earl went directly to the parlor; and on facing the newcomer he gave a start, much more perceptible than the president's had been, and gurgled forth the gasp of astonishment.

Chapter IV

MASTER ETHELRED PRESTON

WE left Father Edmunds rather abruptly, and with an exclamation of astonishment upon his lips.

He had counted upon coming face to face with a small, delicate, fragile, golden-haired child, attired according to the manner of a mama's darling. Instead of all this he found himself facing an overgrown boy, with close-cropped sandy hair, large, coarse, round features, and something very like a cast in the left eye.

This was the instantaneous impression which caused him the involuntary betrayal of his astonishment. A second look embraced further and no less interesting details of the newcomer's personal appearance.

His teeth were large and, as far as they came into evidence, complete. They were very much in evidence, too; for Master Ethelred wore a smile such as nothing but a large mouth and much fatuousness could effect. The appearance of his ears, which projected rather boldly from the head, caused Father Edmunds to regret that the boy's mother had seen fit to allow her Ethelred to be so closely shorn of his ambrosial locks. His nose was small, of an interrogative turn, and so much out of proportion to his mouth as to give the moon-faced youth a comical expression.

Ethelred was standing; and his pose failed to show that he had made any special studies in Delsarte. He had braced himself firmly against the heavy parlor table. His feet were rather far apart, and over his vest his hands held firmly a slouchy felt hat, which, on encountering the president's eye, he began to turn about in his thick heavy fingers, while at the same time his smile, already broad beyond the average, widened a trifle, and disclosed teeth which are rarely seen by people who are not dentists.

"Ethelred Preston, I believe," said the president.

The smile vanished like the passing of a flash of light.

"Yes," came the reply, in the tone of which the pipe of youth struggled with the lower notes of a changing voice, to the manifest disadvantage of both.

Having acquitted himself of this mono-syllable, Ethelred fastened his eyes upon his hat and fell into the fatuous smile with an instantaneousness which rather disconcerted the president. It was as though the light had again reappeared.

"I am glad to see you, Ethelred," continued Father Edmunds, holding out his hand.

Ethelred ceased smiling, and glanced with evident distress first at the proffered hand and then at his hat. His difficulty, as far as Father Edmunds could make it out, was to shake hands and at the same time continue to hold the hat unchanged upon his vest.

Father Edmunds, after an awkward moment, took the hat from Ethelred, greatly to the dear child's relief, and laid it on the table. Then Ethelred shook hands.

"I was under the impression, Ethelred, from the tenor of your mother's letter, and the details which I gleaned from it, that you were a little boy."

Ethelred turned to look at his hat. It was still on the table. He grinned at it; then, facing the president, he said:

"No."

He seemed to get an inspiration from this remark, for he added:

"I was; but I've growed."

"Like a weed?" suggested the president, with a smile which, though accompanying his words, was really evoked by Ethelred's naïve explanation.

"Yes," answered the new Fauntleroy, and he added, "I've growed right smart lately."

"But your mother writes of you as though you were a child of twelve or thirteen."

"I'm fourteen—just."

"Indeed! One would take you to be sixteen, at the very least."

"Yes," assented Ethelred, turning toward his hat, and giving Father Edmunds an opportunity of noticing that his coat was rather loosefitting below the collar. "But I've growed. The old woman," continued the interesting youth, "talks about me same as she used to when I was very small. I've growed right smart lately."

"By the old woman, I take it, you mean your mother?"

"Yes," assented Ethelred stolidly.

"Why don't you call her your mother?"

In answer to this, Ethelred looked at his hat for a moment and, then, in another burst of inspiration, clapped it upon his head.

The president gently removed the hat, apparently to the relief of Ethelred.

"Why do you call her the old woman?" he persisted.

"Because I always call her the old woman. That's so, so help me."

"Do you know Earl Meriwether, Ethelred?"

"Yes—that is, the old w—my mother knows his old—his mother."

During the whole of this animated dialogue Ethelred had gone from smiles to seriousness and from seriousness to smiles. The effect was not unlike the turning on and off of a search light. Before speaking he became solemn of face, and having delivered his remarks, he lapsed into his fatuous grin. For the rest, now that his hat was in Father Edmunds' hand, he moved neither to the right nor the left, but still braced firmly against the table, with legs wide apart, he kept his eyes fastened upon the head-gear, which appeared to have some extraordinary fascination for its owner.

"Well, if you come along with me," said the president, "I shall take you to the prefect of studies to be examined for your class. By the way, you are big enough for the senior department, but acting under the impression left me by your mother's letter of yesterday, I had assigned you to the small boys' division. However, as you are but fourteen, the arrangement may stand. Now come with me, Ethelred."

Ethelred, without changing his position, stood gazing intently and smiling upon the hat.

"Is there anything else, Ethelred?"

"Gimme that hat."

Father Edmunds restrained his features very well as he returned the valuable article to its owner. Ethelred at once put the hat upon his head and then followed Father Edmunds into the passage.

When they arrived at Father Howard's room, Ethelred, before entering after the president, carefully laid his hat midway upon the threshold, which done, he seemed to be somewhat more at his ease.

"Father Howard, this is Ethelred Preston, who proves to be a much bigger boy than we were led to expect. After you have examined him for his class, you might put him in the charge of Earl Meriwether."

"Are you determined to study hard, my boy?" asked Father Howard, taking Ethelred's hand.

"Yes," said Ethelred, and he smiled vacantly at the Father's table.

As the president turned to leave the room, the newcomer awoke from his smiling trance and ejaculated, "Say!" upon which he began fumbling in his inner coat pocket.

"There!" he added, producing a sealed envelope and tendering it to Father Edmunds, "that's for you."

When the president reached his room, he opened the envelope, took out the enclosure, and with blended feelings of amusement and perplexity read the following:

To the President of Henryton College

Sir: This letter will introduce to you Master Ethelred Preston, a boy of a most estimable and cultured family. He is a God-fearing lad, of a very pleasing address, and eminently qualified to enter and adorn any college in the land. It is against my will and my advice that he is sent to a Catholic school, where, nevertheless, I trust that his sweet qualities of heart and his excellent talents will be duly recognized and appreciated.

I regret, too, that, removed thus early from the refining and elevating influence of home, he may possibly lose that happy combination of frankness and urbanity which has thus far been the salient trait of his budding character.

Hoping that he will receive the care and attention to which he is entitled, and trusting that his religious views will not be unduly influenced—as he is a most impressionable child—I am,

Yours respectfully,
Meredith Sherwin
*(Pastor St. George's
Episcopal Church)*

Chapter V

IN WHICH ETHELRED PROPOSES TO RUN AWAY

"WHY, I thought you were a mama's darling!" blurted out Earl, as he shook hands with Ethelred in the parlor.

"I'll bet I ain't!" returned the gifted new-comer. "I'll teach you fellows a trick or two before you're much older. Say, where did you get them cuff-buttons?"

"I bought them," answered Earl, submit-ting his hand to the artless admirer.

"How much?"

"I don't remember; sixty cents, I believe."

"Will you take a quarter for them?"

"I don't want to sell."

"I'll give you thirty cents."

"Are you really anxious to have them?"

"Yes, I am."

"Well, I'll make you a present of them."

"Thanks; you're the kind of a fellow I like to meet. You don't get something for noth-ing very often nowadays. Can I have them right now?"

"Well, you beat any boy I've ever met!" laughed Earl. "You don't think I'm going to run away, do you?"

"No; but you might forget, or change your mind. People often do. I've been fooled that way lots of times. So, if you can give me them now—"

"Wait till dinnertime. We go to the wash-room just before dinner, and then I can get another pair out of my box."

"And you'll stick to your promise?"

"Of course," answered Earl, with a touch of annoyance in his voice.

Meanwhile, Ethelred had been surveying Earl's clothes with undisguised interest. His eyes finally fixed themselves on Earl's chest.

"Got any more neckties like that?" continued Ethelred, unabashed.

"No," said Earl, shortly. "Have you been examined yet for your class?"

"Yes; I'm in Third Commercial."

"What!" gasped Earl. "Haven't you been studying all your life?"

"I guess not. What kind of a school is this anyhow?"

"It's a jail," said Earl, sorely.

He was still chafing under the sense of wounded justice. It was the first time that he had ever been disloyal to his college; and he felt a qualm of conscience almost as soon as he had uttered the remark. He had spoken on impulse, and now that the complaint had been made, he knew that his words were the product of spite and not of reason.

"So they hold you in tight, do they?"

As Ethelred put this question he was carefully examining the various articles of bric-a-brac on the center table.

"Yes: a boy hasn't much liberty here."

"Well, you'll see they won't hold *me* in tight."

"Why, what'll you do?"

Before answering, Ethelred walked over to the door, opened it cautiously and peeped out into the corridor.

"Because," he said, closing the door and advancing dramatically to Earl's side, "because I'm going for to run away. You don't catch me staying in any jail—not if I know it."

Earl was somewhat dismayed. He had not intended to encourage his new charge toward a step so extraordinary and unusual. Nor was he in a mood courageous enough to retreat from the false position into which his comment on the college had placed him. In a word, he was not himself.

"What will your mother do if you run away?" he asked, weakly.

"Her! Oh, she's started for Europe. We've broke up house. *She* won't know the difference."

"Where will you go, then?"

"I have friends—lots of 'em," said Ethelred, darkly. "All I want is about ten dollars to get away on. Can you lend me ten dollars?"

"No. I haven't that much money. Besides, I don't care about helping you to run away, anyhow."

"You said the place was like a jail—didn't you? If you mean to stand by what you said, I don't see why you're not willing to help. Are you afraid to trust me?" Ethelred, as he spoke, put on a very belligerent air.

"Of course, I'm not afraid. But I haven't ten dollars nor anything like that sum. I'm a little short of money just now."

"Well, you could lend me twenty-five cents—couldn't you?"

"All right," said Earl, taking out some silver and selecting a quarter.

Ethelred literally clutched the silver quarter, pocketed it with an appearance of precipitation, and then gazed hungrily at the money still remaining in Earl's fingers.

"Couldn't you lend me a little more?— You've got lots."

Earl could not conceal an expression of annoyance. By way of answer, he handed Ethelred a ten-cent piece and returned the rest of the money to his pocket.

"Oh, come on," urged the new boy, "lend a feller another quarter, can't you?"

"Ethelred Preston," said Earl, looking the beggar straight in the eye, "you're an out-and-out shark."

"Throw in another dime, anyhow," Ethelred pleaded, with outstretched palm.

He might have read disgust in Earl's very emphatic silence, but he did not.

"You're a nice friend, Meriwether! I didn't think you'd be so stingy—"

Here Ethelred, who had fallen into a whining tone, came to a sudden pause. There was something in Earl's flashing eye which cowed him. He added: "Oh, you needn't get mad; I was only fooling. All I wanted of you was a quarter or so. I reckon I can get the rest of the money from some of the other fellers."

"You're pretty cool for a newcomer. Suppose we come outside and take a look at the place."

"All right; nothing like business. I want to know where I am. Say, you'll get me a chance to get to know the fellows"—Ethelred pronounced it "fellers"—"before I run away tomorrow night?"

"Of course," answered Earl, as he threw open the parlor door and the two walked out into the corridor. "There's a half holiday today, as it's Thursday; and I'll introduce you all around."

"Many boys here, Meriwether?"

"There are about sixty in our division, and nearly one hundred and fifty in the Senior Division."

"That so? And where do they all come from?"

"Pretty much from every State in the Union, even from California. Besides, there are several from Mexico, and a few from South America."

"I suppose most of them here are a pretty green lot," continued Ethelred in a loud voice.

There were five or six of the senior students in the corridor, who happened to catch this remark. Then they made some remarks in return, which, luckily for Ethelred's peace of mind, the newcomer did not hear. Before dinnertime, Ethelred's artless speech had been rehearsed to nearly every student, large and small, in Henryton College. These things spread very quickly in boarding schools.

Earl, meantime, answered ironically:

"Oh, yes; boarding-school boys are noted for their greenness."

The irony was lost upon his companion.

"And are the fellows tolerably flush just now?" queried Ethelred in a whisper.

"I can't say, I'm sure. I don't ask my friends how much money they carry."

"But you see I want to borrow some money to get away on. I ain't no fool. You don't catch me running away with nothing in my pockets."

"There! What do you think of that?" cried

Earl, forgetting his vexations and troubles in a burst of admiration, as he and his companion came out upon the steps which commanded a view of the playground and its environs.

It was a sight to win enthusiasm from anyone whose eyes were alive to the beauty of scenery. Before them stretched the cheerful playground, level, unbroken, and shaded at the lower end by a row of noble oaks. To the right and left of the two boys standing on the steps, maples formed its boundaries on either side, and back of these trees, beautiful even in their wintry bareness, lay two stretches of luxuriant lawn, still quite green despite midwinter, whither, with permission of the prefect, the small boy delighted to resort in the short recesses and the intervals between their games. To the west the lawn was bounded by a stone wall some five feet in height; to the east it was cut off from the flower garden of the college by a fence of strong oak palings. Beyond the growth of oaks at the lower end could be seen, here and there, the spires of several village church-steeples; further still many a dainty cottage was visible among the vine-clad hills which stretched away as far as the eye could see; while between the steeples that gleamed in the sunlight and the hills beyond lay, glittering and dimpling and changing, the noble curve of one of America's most beautiful rivers.

Back of the garden stood the infirmary, an ancient building hallowed for its traditions. Over it crept the ivy in its rich-tinted winter livery. It was an excellent playground, framed in as exquisite a setting of scenery as boy or man could desire.

"Isn't that beautiful!" ejaculated Earl. "Just look at the river."

"It looks like silver, doesn't it?" commented the poetic Ethelred. "Say, you won't tell that I'm going to run away, will you?"

"It's none of my business. I think, though, that if you wait long enough you may change your mind. Most of the boys here like the place. I used to like it myself till lately. But things have changed. We'll go over to the stone wall and take a look at the village if you like."

"All right, Earl. The old woman says you're not a Catholic."

"*Who?*"

"The old woman."

"You mean your mother, do you? No, I'm not a Catholic, and I never will be one."

"That's right," said Ethelred, with some enthusiasm; "I hate Catholics myself. They are a narrer set and the enemies of our public institootions. They are ridden by priests, who are most ignorant men, and they would trample in the dust the starry flag for which our fathers bled and suffered and under which Liberty smiles upon a rejoonated world. No sir," he added, dropping from what was evidently a quotation to his usual, elegant speech, "you don't catch me attending at a school where I am thrown in with Catholics."

"You're talking nonsense!" answered Earl indignantly. "The Catholics are not enemies of our public institutions. Who told you that they would trample on our flag? They don't go round parading their patriotism without rhyme or reason like a lot of hypocrites who are not Americans at all. If shouting for the American flag counts, the Catholics would not be at all comparable to some people in America; but when it comes to fighting for the flag, the shouters go to Canada and the Catholics take the field. The idea of *your* talking about not going with Catholic boys! The boys here are gentlemen."

"Aw! I thought you were not a Catholic."

"I'm not. But my best friends are Catholics, and my teachers have all been Catholics, and I'm not such a fool as to believe what a lot of ignoramuses say against people whom I know personally."

"They're idolaters," continued Ethelred, "and—hello! What's this?"

They had reached the stone wall on the eastern side. It rose about four feet and a half above the level of the playground, but on glancing over it, Ethelred was astonished to find that it went down sheer to a depth of thirty feet. Below them lay the northern end of the town.

"We're up pretty high, you see," explained Earl. "It's the same at the lower end of the yard. The wall there goes down about forty feet, and below it is another part of Henryton. The part of the town we see from the steps is the high part near the river. Our college was built on the top of a hill, and now it's pretty hard work to get down to the village. Some of the large boys tried it this year, but they got caught."

"How can a fellow get out of this place, so as to catch the train down there at the depot?"

"By the porter's lodge."

"Yes; but won't he be noticed?"

"Of course; if you want to steal out, you might drop down over this wall," suggested Earl, with a twinkle.

Thus the conversation drifted on, as the

two boys made a leisurely examination of the premises, so that when the bell rang for the end of studies, Ethelred had obtained some few ideas on college life, of which he seemed to know very little, and had been shown the various nooks and corners of the yard, the playroom, the gymnasium and the candy shop. This latter place aroused his enthusiasm. He inquired eagerly into the prices of the various wares, and was particularly anxious to learn the average amount of sales made in a month, a point on which Earl was unable to inform him.

"Why, what small fellers they are!" exclaimed the newcomer as the junior students came flocking from the study hall into the yard.

"That's what they're expected to be," said Earl. "This is the Junior Division, you know. You're the biggest boy on this side, I think."

"I can lick any boy here," said the modest youth, surveying the entire division with the eye of scorn.

"No doubt," answered Earl, dryly.

"Why most of them are in knickerbockers, and a lot of them have baby collars."

"Yes; they are dressed the way boys of their age are usually dressed. How would you expect them to dress? Wear their pants in their boots and carry bowie knives?"

While the two were thus commenting on the appearance of their schoolmates, Devereux and Haines came strolling past them arm in arm. They had heard a part of Ethelred's comments.

"Come over here, Ed and Roger!" called Earl; "I want to introduce you to Ethelred Preston."

"What greenies they are," whispered the knowing Ethelred in Earl's ear, as the two advanced, smiling, to take his hand and bid him welcome. He had intended to couch this animadversion in a whisper, but his voice, as has been said, was in the rudest period of transition, and the whisper was loud enough to be heard by Devereux, the wag of the small yard.

Eddie had already formed his opinion of the newcomer. Ethelred, with his hat perched on the back of his head, his arms akimbo and his mouth somewhat open, looked at once confident and countrified—a combination which, to the small boy who has been for some time at boarding school, invites teasing on sight.

"It's a real pleasure to me to meet you," said Ed, with a smile and a twinkle. "Are you recovered from your grief at leaving the dear ones at home?"

"I'm not a milksop," returned Ethelred, loftily.

"No; neither am I. My name is Ed Devereux and this fellow is Roger Haines. You heard of Webster's reply to Haynes, didn't you?"

"No, I didn't."

"You don't say! Well Roger Haines, though he spells his name somewhat differently, is the uncle of Haynes, the great orator, and his grandfather signed the Declaration of Independence with a blue lead pencil."

"What did he do that for?"

"Sign the Declaration?" asked Ed suavely, while Roger and Earl were struggling to keep their countenances: "Why, he signed it for his health, and he used a blue pencil because he had been brought up that way."

Ethelred glared at Devereux, whose pretty face was all suavity.

"Has Earl shown you the grounds?" continued Ed.

"Yes; he's showed me most everything."

"Did he call your attention to the associations which link this place with the dead and buried past?"

"Do you mean a life insurance company?"

Hereat Roger exploded, and Earl turned away his face.

"What are you laughing at?—confound you!" roared Ethelred.

"He was laughing at what I said about the past," explained Ed. "It is dead, but not buried. But to be serious: if I were you, I wouldn't lean so heavily against that tree."

"Why not?"

Ethelred had braced himself against a large and venerable oak. At Ed's words he straightened up with no little precipitation and turned to look at the huge trunk.

"Because," answered Ed, "that is the very tree to which George Washington tied his horse when he came visiting here."

"Is that so?"

"Oh, very much so indeed. Now just come down this way," said Ed, moving toward the wall at the lower end. "You see that large stone standing a little above the line of the others in the wall?"

"Yes."

"Come on, and get near, so that you can touch it with your hands. You needn't take off your hats, boys; the weather is turning cold. Now this stone is the most precious relic we've got."

"I don't believe in relics," growled Ethelred, with a slight upward turn of his tip-tilted nose.

"You mean in the Catholic sense, I suppose. Catholics honor the bones and garments and the things which belong to those of their dead who were particularly good and holy; but some very fine people who are not Catholics think they are very foolish."

"That's so!" said Ethelred, heartily.

"But Protestants don't mind honoring the remains of dead people, provided that those people were great and famous in the world's eyes. For instance, they'll travel far to see and honor a sword worn by Washington; and if they owned it, they'd put it in a glass case. But they wouldn't care about looking at a bishop's crook to show it reverence, not even if the bishop were the holiest man that ever lived."

"I guess that's about the size of it," returned Ethelred, thoughtfully. He did not quite catch the drift of Eddie's remarks, and so, resolving to change the subject and return to the main question, he continued: "But what about this stone?"

"It's a great relic, as I was saying. You see that place on top where it's so worn? It is worn by the kisses which patriotic Americans have given it."

"What is it?" urged Ethelred, becoming really interested.

"It's the stone on which sat for over two hours, by actual count, the servant of Benedict Arnold, while his master was betraying his country. If you like, you may kiss it, but don't make too much noise about it."

Ethelred gazed at the stone with an air of stupid uncertainty upon his face.

"Better take off your hat, if you want to kiss it," suggested Ed.

When Ethelred uncovered and leaned over to press his lips upon the slab, the boys broke into a roar of laughter.

Ethelred did not kiss the stone. He turned round, and his face was flushed with anger, while there was a look in his eyes that should have petrified Devereux.

But Ed went on laughing, while his companions kept him company. Haines was actually doubled up. Of the three laughers, Earl was the only one who preserved any semblance of self-control.

Then Ethelred gave utterance to some very ugly words, words which do not sound pleasantly to the refined ear and which have not, very fortunately, found their way into even the most ambitious dictionaries. Happily, the laughing trio did not hear them. In fact, Earl was the only one who was watching Ethelred. And it was good that he was, for with a last oath, Ethelred made a dash at Ed with the evident intent of knocking him down.

Earl sprang forward and caught the clenched fist raised to strike his friend.

With more language of the street, Ethelred turned upon Earl.

"I'll do you up!" he shouted.

But here the other two came to the rescue, and the belligerent newcomer was a prisoner.

"You're afraid to fight me!" he foamed. "You're a coward," he added, addressing himself to Devereux, "and I'll thrash the life out of you!"

"Do you really want to fight?" asked Ed.

"You can just bet your life I do!" howled the dear child.

"Am I to understand that you challenge me to a fight?"

"Let me at him!" screamed the pride of his mother, struggling to break loose from Roger and Earl.

"Hold on; keep quiet," said Ed. "I am perfectly willing to fight with you according to college rules. If you promise not to rush at me, they'll let you loose, and then we can arrange the terms."

"Oh, if you're willing to fight, I'll promise. I'm going to teach you a lesson."

"Let him loose, boys. Well, to begin with, we'll fight with gloves—with boxing gloves, in the gymnasium. According to rules here, there's to be no clinching, but it must be boxing all through. Haines and Meriwether will be referees and timekeepers, if you have no objection, and we'll have it out after dinner."

"Can't I catch hold of you and smash you on the ground and wipe up the earth with you?"

"Not much; I shouldn't like that at all. Besides, it's vulgar. That's the way alley rats fight."

"You mean to say I'm an alley rat?"

"Of course not. Well, we'd better go to the washroom, boys, if we want to get a wash before dinner. By the way, Ethelred, don't talk about a *fight* after dinner. Around here we call it a boxing contest. If you call it a fight, the boys will laugh at you."

"I say," said Ethelred to Earl on the way to the washroom, "you haven't forgot about them cuff-buttons, have you?"

Chapter VI

ETHELRED PUTS ON THE BOXING GLOVES

IT cannot have escaped the observation of the reader that Master Ethelred's carriage and language before the students were quite different from those which distinguished him in his interview with the president and vice-president of Henryton. In the company of the students he was easy, but not elegant; in the presence of the faculty he was neither, while his smile was actually a horror to the eye and a trial to the nerves. This smile was Ethelred's idea of "company" manners.

In recording the various pearls of wisdom which, in the course of this narrative, are to fall from Ethelred's lips, the writer takes the liberty of putting down most of Ethelred's words, not as the charming newcomer actually pronounced them, but as he would have pronounced them had he been better acquainted with the prejudices of educated men. The writer also softens, on occasion, the slang, the provincialisms and the variations from received idiom which Ethelred, throughout his interesting college career, let fall with prodigal and artless profusion.

Had Father Edmunds, president of Henryton College, witnessed Earl and Ethelred's meeting, doubtless he would have been puzzled extremely. Even as it was, he was at a loss to account for what little he had seen. In the experiences of long years given to college work, he had met with not a few rude boys whose parents were of ordinary refinement; but in every case, there was always to be discovered in these lads some evidence of their home training. The case of Ethelred seemed to stand alone. The boy in look, in gesture, in carriage, in language, was a boor. There was nothing, so far as externals went, to show that he had known a refined and loving mother's care, nothing which would lead one to suppose that he had ever before entered a parlor.

In the vice president's room, as Father Howard had subsequently deposed to the president, Ethelred had gone on smiling in the same silly way. When he had no answer, he smiled; before answering, he smiled; after answering, he smiled again; then *da capo*. The interview over, he seemed to find it impossible to leave the room. However, the student who does not know how and when to bow himself out is to be found not infrequently among those who make some pretensions to manners.

If anything, a new complication was added to the mystery of Master Ethelred's want of politeness by the letter from the boy's pastor, who, as we have seen, enlarged upon Ethelred's sweetness and nobility. Against the witness of pastor and mother was the boy himself.

While Father Edmunds sits in his study, turning over all these things, there comes by the noon mail another letter, which satisfies him that the problem is not insoluble.

> Mayor's Office
> Brighton, January 28, 189-
> REVEREND EDMUND EDMUNDS

Dear Sir: Mrs. Preston has requested me to send you a word of recommendation in regard to her only child now intrusted to your charge. I have to say, he is a good boy, will appreciate kind treatment, and is of excellent talents.

I feel bound to tell you, however, that he left for your school in a fret and a very rebellious mood. Some of the boys here have told him dreadful stories of Catholic schools, and, besides, he does not want to leave his mother. He threatened to run away before leaving home, so keep an eye on him. Once he feels at home, you will find him a good, docile boy.

> Yours truly,
> James Hickson Dodge,
> *Mayor of Brighton*

"Ah," reflected the president, "this explains much, if it does not cover the whole case. For all I know, the boy, while in my presence, may have been looking to see whether I wore hoofs. No wonder his manners were so poor. That hideous smile of his must have come from pure nervousness. Coming here in such a frame of mind, it is but natural that he should show the rough corners of his character. Well, I will not judge him yet."

And he at once went to the vice president's room to hand him the mayor's letter.

In the small boys' dining hall, meantime, Ethelred was assigned a seat at the table over which Earl Meriwether presided. A whisper had gone round among the lads in the washroom that the newcomer was his mama's darling, and at once he was christened "Darling."

Blessed with a very good appetite, Ethelred was rather original in his methods of satisfying it. If he wanted something, he stood up and reached for it, and his eagerness in getting the food which he desired was artlessly exhibited. "Hurry up with that potato dish, can't you?" he growled at his neighbor, Peter Lane, a tiny, weazen-faced youth with small, bright eyes.

"Say 'please,'" answered Peter, holding back the dish and gazing up pertly into the big fellow's face.

Armed with his fork, the Darling reached forward and stabbed a potato.

"Oh-h-h-h!" came a chorus of mock horror from eight of the ten lads seated around the table. Their groaning was cut short by the ringing of a small hand bell.

Paying no attention to the sound, the Darling bellowed out, "My meals is paid for!" A silence had fallen upon the refectory at the bell's tinkle, and this speech fell upon over one hundred and twenty merry ears, the owners of which at once broke into a jolly laugh.

"Sh!" hissed Earl in the Darling's ear. "Look over there."

Ethelred, who had just stabbed another potato with his fork, turned and saw the prefect, who was standing beside the reader's desk and gazing at him with a countenance of disapproval. On catching the boy's eye, the prefect put his finger to his lip.

"Can't we talk, Earl?" he croaked—the nearest thing to a whisper within the range of his voice.

"No; that boy on the stand over there is going to read. We're supposed to listen while we eat."

"'The Badgers of Belmont,' by Maurice Francis Egan," cried the reader.

"I've seen badgers in a menagerie," croaked the Darling to Earl. "Have you ever—"

"Sh!" hissed Earl, who, in common with all the youngsters, was deeply interested in the fates and fortunes of the jolly little Badgers.

Luckily for Ethelred he was hungry; so, consenting to hold his tongue provisionally, he addressed himself to the contents of his plate and for the most part bolted his food. When he wanted anything, he reached for it, or if that were out of the question, he got up from his chair and went for it. This latter performance happened three different times before the prefect whispered something into his ear. Thereafter he would nudge his neighbor when he desired anything and, having thus secured his attention, would point gravely with his knife or fork, as was more convenient, at the dish which he then happened to want. Thus far, in his college career of a few hours, he had done nothing to secure the respect of anyone.

On finishing his meal, which, considering his hearty appetite, he accomplished with a promptness and despatch wonderful to behold, he put a toothpick into his mouth and employed the remaining time spent in the dining hall in examining with lively satisfaction the pair of cuff-buttons which Earl had given him.

"Mr. Conway," said Ed Devereux to the second prefect after dinner, "we're going to have a little fun in the gymnasium. Darling—that is, Ethelred Preston, wanted to fight me, and I told him I'd do it with boxing gloves. There will be two fellows to see we don't clinch, and so there'll be no harm done. It will be an ordinary boxing match. The fun of it is that the Darling thinks it a regular fight to a finish."

As Eddie, a moment later, entered the gymnasium, he glanced about with a flush of pleasure upon a scene that was almost picturesque. The center of the gymnasium was shut off from view by a circle of boys. Above them, upon trapeze and ladder and horizontal bar, were perched the more restless. Within the ring were Earl and Roger Haines engaged in dressing the Darling for the contest.

Roger took the liberty of feeling Ethelred's muscles. He gasped with affected astonishment.

"Oh, what a biceps!" he cried. Then one

by one, and in perfect order, the young gentlemen who had formed the ring advanced and touched, with exaggerated reverence, the Darling's arm.

"He doesn't eat potatoes by the forkful for nothing!" piped Peter from his perch on the trapeze.

Ethelred, who had been strutting about like a fighting cock and receiving these attentions with ridiculous complacency, flushed angrily at the remark.

"You little fool!" he exclaimed above the laughter caused by Peter's remark, "I'll pay you back for this before night."

"Go on and put on your gloves," said Devereux. "Say, boys," he whispered to two or three, "pass round the word to make the circle wider and give me lots of room just as soon as we put up our hands."

Some delay was occasioned by the unsuccessful attempt of the Darling, at the suggestion of Roger Haines, to turn his gloves inside out before putting them on.

Roger grinned and, slipping over to Ed, whispered, "He couldn't tell a boxing glove from an air pump. Just keep him away from you and there'll be no trouble."

At length the two were ready and stepped into the ring—Ed, small, light, wiry; the Darling, heavy, ungainly, three inches taller and at least thirty pounds heavier.

The two shook hands and took position.

"Ready!" cried Earl. "Go!"

Forthwith, putting his head down, Ethelred's hands began to work like the arms of a windmill, and his blows came raining continuously upon the very place where Eddie's merry face had been when he directed them. But Eddie's feet were quicker than the Darling's arms; he was dancing what looked very like a jig and, at the same time, warding off the blows with an ease which indicated the practiced boxer. For two minutes the rain beat; for two minutes the dancer danced. Then suddenly a slight arm shot through Ethelred's guard, and a very soft glove came in contact with Ethelred's nose. It did not hurt, but it roused the enthusiasm of the boys and the Darling's anger. The rain became fiercer than ever, while Eddie faster than ever danced round and round the ring; but it was a rain which did not fall on the ground which it was intended to reach. So far as the Darling's intentions were concerned, the rain was a drought. Just before the end of the three minutes, the tiny right arm shot out again and the glove touched the same spot for the second time. On this occasion it hurt just the least little bit. Time was called, finding Ed smiling radiantly, Ethelred breathing heavily.

"You don't fight fair," panted the latter. "Why don't you stand still?"

"And wait till you hit me?"

"Yes; but just wait till next round! I'll learn you a lesson. You'll know who you're talking to next time."

"To Mama's Darling!" sang out Peter from on high.

In the next round the rain did not fall quite so heavily. Ethelred's animation seemed to have been transferred from his arms to his breathing, which had become very heavy and very rapid, and the light hand found Ethelred's nose accurately three times out of five attempts. Then the Darling attempted to clinch, but was promptly restrained by the referees. In the third minute of this round, Eddie struck out with unusual vivacity.

"Time—blood!" called out Haines. "That ends it," added Earl. "In our contests here, all we want is blood, and when we get that we're satisfied. Ethelred, you're beaten."

"I've been tricked!" growled Ethelred, whose nose bleeding had been of the most transient character. "You don't call that sort of thing a fight, do you?"

"Of course not," assented Earl. "It's a contest; we don't fight, and you've got the worst of it. Now shake hands with Devereux."

"No; I won't."

"Oh-h-h-h!" cried the crowd, in mock horror.

Shamed into submission, Ethelred shook hands and hurried from the room into the yard.

As events proved, it would, in all probability, have been better for him had he remained in the gymnasium.

Chapter VII

ETHELRED IN THE FRYING PAN

WHEN Ethelred entered the yard, it was deserted. He shivered; for the change from the warm, comfortable gymnasium to the northerly breeze without is likely to be appreciated by one who has just come forth from a boxing contest. Under other circumstances, he might have been tempted to return; but just now he wanted a little solitude, for he was beginning to fancy that the boys had been playing upon him. However, he was not dismayed. His turn was to come yet. As he had intimated publicly on several distinct occasions, he would teach these college boys that he could not be imposed upon.

While walking up and down the yard, he counted his money.

"Two dollars and eighty-five cents," he said. "That's good for a beginning. I'll have ten dollars by tomorrow noon."

Returning the money to his pocket, he walked toward that end of the yard which gave a view of the Senior Division's playgrounds.

Ten or twelve large boys were standing at the boundaries nearest him. They returned his survey with considerable interest and held a whispered consultation.

Ethelred, after gazing at the group for a moment, thought well to step over and have a talk.

"Look a-here," he began. "I notice that some of you chaps ain't any bigger than me. How is it that you fellows are in the big yard, and me in the little?"

"Professor Salvini," said the smallest student in the group as he turned toward a serious-faced young man with a slight mustache, "perhaps you can explain this. Are you aware that this newcomer has been put in the small yard?"

The person addressed as Professor Salvini was Edward Land, a student of Philosophy. He combined the dignity of a professor with a student's love of fun. Stroking his mustache, and eyeing Ethelred very sternly, he said in a solemn baritone:

"Your name, my son?"

"Ethelred Preston."

"How long is it since you were born?"

"Excuse me, professor," put in the first speaker, "I wish to call Professor Petersol."

And before turning upon his heel, he raised his hat with great reverence.

"I'm near sixteen, if that's what you mean," answered Ethelred, relapsing into the smile which had unnerved the president.

"See here, don't laugh unless I tell you. Have you got your baptismal certificate about you?"

"No," answered Ethelred, whose face was now very grave.

"Well, let that pass. What's your name?"

"Ethelred Preston."

"Let me see," mused Professor Salvini, taking out a notebook. "Oh, yes, you came here today. The president received you, I believe. Who told you to go into the Junior Division?"

"The president and the vice president both."

"There!" exclaimed the professor with much vehemence, addressing the solemn and attentive crowd about him. "Those two are always interfering with my authority. Ethelred Preston, why didn't you come to me?"

"I—I didn't know."

"But you should have known, sir. Ah, here comes Professor Petersol. I shall have to confer with him."

Accompanied by the boy who had recently left the group, there now approached a tall, thin, cadaverous young man who could not have been more than twenty. His face was very serious and solemn. As he came near, all the boys raised their hats.

"We can never have perfect discipline in this college," he said in strong, resolute tones, "till the president and vice president learn their places. Where is the newcomer?"

"Here he is, sir."

"This is the fellow, sir," came the chorus from the bystanders.

Professor Petersol folded his arms, threw his head back, and said:

"Let him be presented."

"Professor Petersol," said Professor Salvini, "allow me to introduce you to Ethelred Stampton."

"It's Preston, sir," suggested one of the group.

"That," returned Professor Salvini, "remains to be proved. As the boy has no baptismal record, and as, on the other hand, the difference between 'pressed on' and 'stamped on' is practically nothing, at least from the point of view of a football player, I shall stick to my first introduction and repeat, Professor Petersol, allow me to introduce you to Ethelred Stampton."

With his head still high in the air, his arms folded, the professor looked down from his lofty height upon Ethelred. Ethelred looked up and grinned.

"Take off your hat, sir!" roared Professor Petersol. "Never dare to look me in the eye with your hat on. What business," he continued when Ethelred had removed his hat with a little precipitation, "have you over in the Junior Division?"

"I was sent there by the president and vice president."

"Say 'sir' when you address me," commanded Professor Petersol. "The manners of the rising generation are simply deplorable."

Some members of the group were beginning to snicker.

"Boys!" continued Professor Petersol, "what

do you mean by standing around when I am conducting an examination? Get away from here at once."

The students addressed had nothing for it but to go away. They went very unwillingly.

"And I say, James Ellis!" cried out the professor to one of the last of the group, "I'll hear your one hundred lines of memory lesson after I have done with this young man. Smoking on the sly must stop in this college."

Now James Ellis was a member of the graduating class, prefect of the sodality and a student who had never received lines since his entrance at college; whereas, the young man who, for the time being, was addressed as Professor Petersol had just been called away from the memorizing of lines to attend to Ethelred. The professor's remarks to Ellis were too much for the departing crowd, and if Ethelred had not been dazed by Petersol's magnificent assumption of authority, he might have perceived that he was being made the victim of a new practical joke.

"Professor Petersol," resumed Professor Salvini, "don't you think our young friend should be placed in the Senior Division?"

"Assuredly; write out an order on the president to that effect while I question the youth further. Boy, in what class were you placed?"

"In the Third Commercial."

"Put on your hat, my son; the weather is a trifle keen. But think of your being put in the Third Commercial! Who examined you?"

"Father Howard."

"Absurd," put in Professor Salvini. We must discharge Father Howard, and I'm beginning to fear that the president must go too."

"How much time did he spend in examining you?" resumed Professor Petersol.

"About ten minutes."

"Monstrous! Why doesn't the vice president attend to his own business, which he doesn't know, and send boys to be examined to me? He should have taken at least four hours. Professor Salvini, write a note to Father Howard stating that we hold his examination null and void."

Professor Salvini, notebook in hand, continued to write industriously. The senior playground, while this conversation was going on, had almost suddenly become alive with boys, who were all walking up and down in groups of two and three. These various groups contrived to pass at short intervals the trio. From the professors and Ethelred down to the liveliest boy upon the grounds, there was not a single one whose face, so long, at least, as its owner was within sight and hearing of Ethelred, was not set in unutterable gravity.

"Now, boy," resumed Petersol, "follow us to the senior study hall; and be careful on the way thither to observe that gravity of deportment which you see on the faces of the circumambient students; a gravity, I may add, which speaks well for the habits of self-control contracted by the severe training of our college curriculum."

Taking the thoroughly mystified Ethelred by the hand, Professor Petersol walked gravely toward the study hall, exhorting the newcomer in a loud voice, the while, to be extremely careful in the choice of his friends and to apply himself from the outset with diligence to his studies, while Professor Salvini hurried on before them to give warning to the students who might happen to be in the study hall.

When the unhappy pupil and his mentor entered, there were fourteen or fifteen of the seniors at their desks, all of whom turned to gaze upon Ethelred.

On half-holidays, the members of the Senior Division were allowed the privilege of the study room, with the understanding that there was to be no loud talking or boisterous conduct.

Professor Petersol, having conducted Ethelred to a seat near the door, handed him a copy of Cicero.

"The most important qualification in a young student," he observed, "is ability to memorize. Here you have Cicero's celebrated oration, *Pro Marcello*, the opening sentence of which our giddier pupils love to sing to the air of 'Home, sweet home.' You will now take the first hundred lines of this celebrated oration and memorize it within an hour's time."

"But I don't know no Latin," whispered Ethelred. "I can't learn that stuff."

"To learn Latin, the less you know about it the better. Before you begin, I desire to give you a few instructions. First of all, you are to be promoted to the large yard tonight—not before. When the recess begins after the second hour of studies, you will slip over quietly from the Junior Division to the place where you had the high honor of first making my acquaintance. Do you understand?"

"Yes."

At this answer Professor Petersol's face grew black.

"Yes, sir."

"That's better, though you might have said, 'Yes, professor.' In the meantime, you must

tell none of the small boys that you are coming over to our—to this side. They might
become jealous. After you have learned your
memory lesson, you will return to the small
boys and play with them and eat with them,
and spend your two hours of study in their
hall. Now go to work at your memory lesson, and don't you dare to raise your head
from your book till I give the sign."

And then Professor Petersol paraded up
and down the aisles with the airs, much
exaggerated, of a *bona fide* professor, while
Ethelred gazed helplessly upon the book,
while the hall quietly filled with students,
while the silence was such that the slight-
est sound disturbed it. If Ethelred had but
looked around and gazed upon these silent
students, he would doubtless have been puzzled by their facial expression.

Most of them, all agrin, were eyeing him
uninterruptedly; some, red-faced and quivering, were struggling manfully against the
temptation to laugh aloud; and occasionally
one or another would rush incontinently from
the hall to give vent to his emotions outside. Professor Petersol's face, in the meantime, never for a moment relaxed from its
austere gravity.

Something over a quarter of an hour had

gone by when a student came in rather hurriedly and whispered a few words in Professor Petersol's ear; whereupon, forgetting his decorum, the self-appointed study keeper hurried over to Ethelred.

"Boy," he said, "slip back to your yard at once—or our plans for bringing you into this division tonight will be spoiled. Slip out by this door, and be sure not to breathe a syllable to anyone. I excuse you from your memory lesson."

Ethelred, nothing loath, took his leave. The professor followed him by the same door; and his tall form had hardly disappeared when there entered from the opposite entrance the prefect of the division.

To find one hundred and twenty boys out of a possible one hundred and fifty in perfect silence and at their books was something so astonishing that the prefect gave a little start, while his face expressed sincere astonishment.

The boys could hold in no longer—a rich wave of genuine and uncontrollable laughter rolled through the hall.

The prefect at once understood that something out of the ordinary had been going on. He waited quietly till the laughter had subsided and then smilingly rapped with his keys on the door for all to leave.

Immediately, once they were outside the study hall, there formed a group about him to tell him of Professor Petersol and the new-comer. They told the whole story with such evident enjoyment, taking care to inform the prefect that the boy had defied anyone to take him in, that Mr. Evans relished the joke almost as much as the narrators.

I said that they told the whole story. This is not quite correct. They failed to mention that at last recess after night studies Ethelred was to be transferred to the Senior Division.

Perhaps they forgot to mention it.

Chapter VIII

IN WHICH ED DEVEREUX PROPOSES TO HELP ETHELRED RUN AWAY

SHORTLY after Ethelred's departure from the gymnasium, Earl asked Eddie Devereux to take a walk with him outside.

"Ed," he began, when they had gone in

silence halfway across the yard, "I feel pretty bad."

"About Mr. Gade?"

"Not exactly. I feel bad about that too, or rather angry. It seems to me that Mr. Gade has been very harsh and unjust."

"Well, you know, Earl, you haven't been at all up in your lessons for two or three weeks; and up to this you never missed. All the boys have noticed it."

"Well, there are some things a boy can't talk about, Ed. But I want to tell you that I've honestly tried to study lately. But it has been so hard. Up to the retreat I found study so easy. But somehow, since then, my mind goes wool-gathering all the time. I wish you'd pray for me, Eddie. Today I've felt as if I were in danger of going wrong. I actually hate Mr. Gade, and I know that I'm just full of spite. I didn't think that I was that kind of a boy."

"You're not, Earl. This trouble with Mr. Gade will blow over in a couple of days and you'll be the same as ever."

"I'm afraid not. And today I said something that has bothered me ever since. I told the newcomer that this place was a jail. That was disloyal to our college. I've always been treated well here and have had a pretty cheerful time of it; and now the very first time a newcomer is put in my charge, I begin by running the place down."

"A good many fellows say things like that about the place, Earl, and some of them really mean it, too. Is that what is bothering you?"

"That's not all. I had a chance to take back what I said, but I was too mulish or too weak to do it. And then the boy said that he wasn't going to stay in a jail, and he'd run away tomorrow night. You see, in all probability, I've put it into his head to run away."

"But you can stop that, if you want to."

"No; I promised not to interfere, and what is worse, I have lent him money to go away on."

With serious brow, Eddie reflected for some moments. Presently he broke into a grin.

"Good gracious! It's just the thing! Look here, Earl—that fellow has no business at this college. His mother may be a lady, as you say; but he certainly is a street boy. I'm just as sure as can be that if he stays here for a week he will be dismissed or expelled. If you and I were to tell the vice president what we know about him, Ethelred would go by the train tonight. Of course, we don't like to go reporting on a fellow, unless it is really necessary. Now, instead of that, suppose we help him to run away."

"What!" cried Earl.

"Yes, why not? If the president knew the kind of a boy he was, he'd acknowledge that we were doing the college a real service. Now, look; we've got to do one thing or the other—report Ethelred as being unfit to go with the boys here, or help him run away. Don't you think we could help him? It doesn't seem wrong in this case because the president would want him to go too if he knew as much about him as we do; and besides,"— here Ed's eyes glittered—"there'll be lots of fun."

"But," objected Earl, "the boy may not be able to take care of himself. You know his father is in Europe, and his mother is on the way there. If anything were to happen to him, I should feel responsible."

Again Ed fell into thought.

"That's so," he assented. "Can't we get over that difficulty? Of course it would be wrong to help the fellow off if we didn't know he'd be cared for when he got away. I wish we could see our way out of that."

"I remember now," said Earl, "that he said he had lots of friends."

"Did he? Well, I'll tell you what we'll do. We'll find out whether he will go back to people who have a right to care for him. And if he will, then we'll be doing a good act to help him off."

"It will be a good thing for the boys here, certainly," said Earl.

"Yes, and it will do no harm to anyone else. There's not a boy in our yard, as far as I know, who has the least temptation to run away, so there won't be any scandal in the case. They will look upon it as being about the sort of thing which they might expect from a boy like the Darling."

"What has become of him, I wonder? He left the playroom some time ago, and he certainly is not in the yard."

Eddie chuckled.

"I'm willing to bet that he has fallen into the hands of the big boys. I think they've heard about him already. Our refectory reader had a chance to give the reader in the big boy's refectory a few points on the newcomer at second table."

Eddie had rightly guessed the fact, though the cause he assigned was defective. It is true the small boy reader had given his senior confrere an account of Ethelred; but, besides this, every student in the Senior

Division had heard and canvassed Ethelred's remark on the "greenness" of the students. The large boys, by tacit agreement, had resolved to show Ethelred that, along with the simplicity of the dove which distinguished the boarders of Henryton College, there was also the cunning of a few serpents.

The students of Henryton were, as a rule, kind and considerate in their dealings with newcomers. However, if a boy during the first days of his arrival proved himself to be somewhat forward, or plumed himself upon his superior knowledge of life, or gave evidences of being annoyingly conceited, they were not slow in devising plans to bring him to a sense of his position. On rare occasions, moreover, they imposed upon a newcomer for no other reason than a love of harmless fun.

Earl and Eddie were still talking of the new arrival when that worthy came running around the corner of the classroom building.

"Hey there, Darling! You've been out of bounds," called Ed.

Ethelred looked around to see whether any others had noticed his return and then joined the two friends.

"What were you doing in the large yard?" asked Ed.

With a knowing look, Ethelred put his fin-

ger under his right eye and pressed down
upon his cheek, so as to give the two boys
a good view of that organ.

"Do you see any green in my eye?"

"Oh, if you don't care to talk, all right. I
was going to ask you whether they had shown
you the tree next to the one which George
Washington cut with his little hatchet."

"You think you're smart," snarled the Darling. "But I'm going to show you a point or
two before I go tomorrow night."

"Go where?"

"Away from here. Say, can't you lend a fellow a dollar? I don't want to go away without I have some money."

"See here, Ethelred Preston," put in Earl,
"we won't help you to run away unless we
know that you're going home."

"The old w—my mother has gone to
Europe."

"Then we'll not let you run away. You have
no right to leave this college unless you have
a fixed home and someone to take care of
you."

"What business is that of yours?" cried
Ethelred, angrily. He had doubled up his
fists as though he were about to attack Earl.

"I'm going to make it my business. It was
my fault, for all I know, that you got it into

your head to run away; but if you get away it will be my fault too."

"I'd like to know who'll stop me!" roared the Darling.

"I will," answered Earl quietly.

The two boys, as they stood facing each other, formed a striking contrast: Ethelred blustering, passionate, noisy; Earl quiet, cool, determined. Earl's eyes, as he said "I will," fell full upon Ethelred's. The latter bore the gaze for a moment, then turned his head away. A moment before, Ethelred had mentally resolved to "fight" Earl; in that mutual gaze the fight had taken place, and Ethelred was worsted.

"Since you fellows meddle so confoundedly, I don't mind telling you that the old—my mother put me in the charge of Mr. Dodge, the Mayor of Brighton, and told me that if I didn't like this college, after a day or so, I might go away and stay with him."

"Oh!" cried Eddie, greatly relieved, "that makes things better."

"But," objected Earl, "why don't you go to the president of the college, like a man, and tell him you have permission from your mother to leave."

"Because," answered Ethelred, after a pause, "I've lost the letter she gave me to the president. In that there letter she told him to let me go any time I wanted to."

Eddie Devereux grinned.

"You compose nicely," he said.

"If I was to go to the president," pursued Ethelred, who failed to perceive the point of Eddie's remark, "and ask him for to let me go, he'd have to write to the Mayor and wait for an answer, and I'd have to stay here for two or three days longer."

"That would be very hard on you—and some of us too—wouldn't it?" said Eddie. "Well," he continued, "I for one am willing to help you if you'll give your solemn promise to go back to your guardian."

"I'll swear it—I'll take an oath—" Here Ethelred actually began to swear that he would return directly to his guardian, but Earl cut him short.

"All we want is your word of honor."

Ethelred gave his word of honor in five or six varieties. Like many people who set little value on their word, he was most eloquent and facile in promising and in attesting to the truth of his own statements.

"Here's seventy-five cents," said Eddie. "You needn't pay it back unless you come back again."

Ethelred's manner changed at once; he

was now fawning. Money seemed to be the one thing upon which he set value. Earl and Eddie exchanged looks of disgust as the Darling cringed before them. Earl was strongly tempted to leave the sordid newcomer and have nothing more to do with him. He was a noble character and could neither understand nor enjoy such an exhibition of vulgarity. Eddie, on the other hand, had a keen sense of fun. Under all the vulgarity, he saw great promise of future frolic.

"Have you made up your mind as to which way you'll get out?" he asked.

"Not yet, Eddie."

"Why not drop over the wall? It's only thirty feet or so at the east end of the yard."

"Think I want to break my legs?"

"That's so; a runaway with broken legs would be a—" Eddie paused for the phrase.

"A contradiction in terms," supplied Earl.

"We might have three or four fellows below to hold a net to catch you in, the way they do in a circus," Eddie went on.

"No, you don't," said the Darling.

As they spoke, they had walked over to the wall.

"It wouldn't be a bad plan, though; only, the great trouble would be that we'd have to get the four fellows out there to catch you. Oh, I declare! Here's just the place. You see this place where there are a few stones on top loose? We can take them out easily, and we'll let down a rope and hold it till you're down in the street. You can climb down a rope, can't you?"

"Yes, I suppose so."

"Of course you can. And if your muscle gives out, you can twine your legs around the rope and slide down. We can hitch the end of the rope to that tree over there, and Earl and I and Haines will hold it besides. Of course, we won't tell the other fellows about it, but we must have a third person to hold the rope, and Haines will be the very best."

"Where are you going to get the rope?" asked Ethelred.

"Oh, there will be no trouble about that. We've got a tremendous coil of rope in the gymnasium; and I'll see to that myself. Now, the next question is, when do you intend to go?"

"Tomorrow night, so as to catch the train."

"Very good. After second hour's studies there are twenty-five minutes to spare, and we can do it easily. It will be dark then and I'll have the rope here. We'll all come over— Earl, you, Haines and myself—from different parts of the yard, so as not to attract attention."

"But maybe I'll be put in the big yard tomorrow."

Eddie gave Earl a quick side look, and as he did so there was a world of merriment in his eye, for he divined from Ethelred's remark that the senior students too had the hapless newcomer in hand.

"No matter," he said, turning with a perfectly serious face to Ethelred; "you can slip over here just the same. We'll tie the rope in a jiffy, and over you go."

"All right, but I need more money."

"No, you don't; its only sixty miles or so to Brighton."

"Yes; but I want to take a sleeper too, and that costs money."

"How much money have you?"

"Only one dollar and fifty cents, so help—"

"That's not true!" cried Earl.

"I'll swear—"

"Hold on," interposed Earl, "you needn't lie about it. You've been imposing on some of the little boys here and have got one or two dollars out of them. We all know about it."

Ethelred was silent.

"And we want you to let them alone after

this. If we catch you borrowing any more money, we'll let you take care of yourself, and we'll see besides that you pay up before you go."

"I intend to pay back every cent!" protested Ethelred.

"So much the better. Well, remember tomorrow night. There come the boys for a game of football. Did you ever see a game?"

"No."

"Come on, then. I'll explain it to you as you look on."

For the rest of that afternoon, Ethelred, under Earl's care, met with no misadventure.

Chapter IX

*IN WHICH ETHELRED FINDS IT HARD
TO SLEEP UNDISTURBED*

"I WONDER whether he intends to come," said Professor Petersol, better known as Peter Sullivan, to Edward Land, the other pseudo-professor.

"I think so. He has no idea of a college

nor of college boys; and if he has been quiet thus far, no one will be likely to enlighten him."

The two were standing at the appointed spot awaiting Ethelred. It was a dark night, and the wind sweeping down from the north in icy blasts made the place very uncomfortable for a rendezvous. The thermometer, steadily falling throughout the day, was now very near to the zero mark. The two were chafing their ears and stamping their feet upon the ground.

"Isn't it getting cold?" asked Sullivan. "If he doesn't come pretty quick, I'll clear out. A joke's a good thing, but I don't propose to freeze to death for the sake of a laugh."

"But it will be rich. I hope our friend Mr. Hale will not take it amiss."

"I don't see why he should; he likes a joke himself. If he thinks he can present me with a package of cigarettes with sawdust inside of them without my getting back at him, he's mistaken."

"And I haven't forgotten the time when he sent me a box of cigars, upper row all right and the rest of it a collection of tracts on the evil of using fermented wine."

"There's hardly a boy of the upper classes," continued Land, "that he hasn't worked in one way or other. That bottle of anti-fat which came to Fatty Archibald on his last birthday has been traced to Mr. Hale."

"Is that so? Last time he played a practical joke on me, he told me that, if I ever got the chance, I might return him the favor, and now—oh, here comes the victim!"

Breathing heavily, Ethelred at this point joined them.

"What's the matter? You are out of breath, my son," said Sullivan.

"I had a little trouble to get away."

Ethelred did not think it best to go into details. Before leaving the Junior Division, he had thought proper to mete out vengeance upon Peter Lane.

Hurrying from the study hall, and waiting for little Peter to pass, he followed him till they were in a part of the yard where shadows were thickest, and then, catching the little man, proceeded to shake him with all his strength. Had Ethelred been content to nourish his design in secret, all would have gone well for him and ill for Peter; but he had hinted his plan earlier in the evening to Earl, who, in consequence, was on the lookout.

He had scarcely put hands upon Peter, when he was seized by a strong pair of arms from behind and jerked backwards with a force that brought his jaws together with a force that would have given nine students out of ten a violent headache. It did not affect Ethelred in that way, however, but it made him feel decidedly uncomfortable.

"Run off, Peter," said Earl. He continued as Peter disappeared from view: "Ethelred, you're a coward. The idea of picking on the smallest boy in the yard! If you go on this way, there's not a boy here will have anything to do with you."

"I don't care; let go of me, will you; let go—I won't touch him—Ow-w—stop squeezing!"

Released, Ethelred rubbed his arms. They were destined to show blue marks for a week in consequence of the squeeze. Earl, strong above his years and weight, had a grip that was extraordinary.

"Well, good night," said Earl shortly, turning on his heel.

Ethelred paused to invoke some—let us say—blessings on Earl's head, and then, suddenly remembering his appointment, hastened away. All these things, it is hardly necessary to say, the pseudo-professors learned only on the following morning.

"Well, my son," said Edward, "we find on

examination that it won't do for you to go to sleep in the dormitory tonight. Some of the young gentlemen here will become jealous of you, unless we prepare the way gently for your promotion to the Senior Division. Your admission, accordingly, to the Senior Division must be kept a secret till tomorrow afternoon, or possibly till tomorrow night."

"Yes," said Ethelred.

"So we have decided to allow you a private sleeping room for this night. Come on at once, and don't talk on the way."

Crossing the yard, they came to the infirmary building. It was a long, low structure two stories in height, with the windows of the first floor about nine feet above the ground. Avoiding the entrance, Ethelred's guides conducted him to a ladder below the third window on the western side.

"Now, be very quiet," whispered Sullivan, "we want no one to know that you are here— else they might try to play tricks on you. Follow me up the ladder into this room."

Sullivan mounted, followed by Ethelred and Edward.

The room was exquisitely fitted up. A student's lamp upon the center table was alight at the time that they entered and threw a softened splendor upon the entire room. There were tidies, silk hangings, doilies, lace pillowslips, silken curtains, books selected seemingly for their pretty covers and, upon the toilet table, a number of dainty articles.

"How do you like this?" asked Sullivan, removing the rose-colored shade from the lamp.

For answer, Ethelred gazed about him open-mouthed.

"Now, boy, you are to touch nothing in this room except the lamp, which you will blow out as soon as you have undressed; and then go to bed, and stay there till we come for you tomorrow morning."

"Yes, sir."

"If any people should come in here during the night, don't you let them impose on you. However, there does not seem to be much danger. The door, you will observe, is locked. When Professor Salvini and I go, which we shall do by means of the window, so as to keep your being here a secret from the boys, many of whom I regret to say are frivolous, we shall take away the stepladder. So you ought to be quite safe from intruders. Still, if anyone should come in, don't let him impose upon you."

"I'll bet I won't. They're not going to fool *me!*"

"Good night, boy. Go to bed." And the two professors departed by the window.

One hour later, Mr. Hale, who had been downtown to see certain friends of his, returned "carolling lightly" to his room in the infirmary. Mr. Hale was a tall, willowy, young exquisite of twenty-one, with a light mustache, a delicate complexion and a dainty cane. He wore an abundance of rings. Despite appearances, he was a sensible young man who gave pleasure to many by his kindly ways and, with the trifling exception of one or two upon whom he had played practical jokes, offense to none. He resided at Henryton College in the capacity of teacher of flute and piano.

Unlocking himself into his room, he lighted the lamp, took off his coat and put a cigar in his mouth. It was his custom before retiring to while away an hour over a mild Havana. Having struck a match and settled into his armchair, he waited for the blue flame to burn away. And while he was thus waiting, his jaw dropped, his eyes opened wide, he jumped from his chair with a start and was in two minds about rushing from the room.

Beside the bed was a chair on which were piled a shirt, trousers, coat and vest. Upon the pillow—*his* beautiful lace pillow—lay a strange head.

After breathing hard for a minute, Mr. Hale with trembling fingers struck another match, lighted his lamp and, arming himself with his cane, resolved to explore this mystery.

"Hey!" he cried, entrenched behind his chair and standing at a safe distance from the bed. "Wake up there! Who are you?"

Master Ethelred tossed uneasily, gave a groan and was still again.

"Hey there! Wake up. Do you hear?"

No attention was paid to these remonstrances.

Then Mr. Hale did what was for him a bold thing. Stooping down, he picked up a slipper from under his washstand and tossed it lightly into the air. It fell, striking the sleeper's neck.

Ethelred, rubbing his eyes, sat up in bed.

"What are you doing in this room, sir?" stuttered Mr. Hale.

"None of your business. You just clear out of here and let me alone."

"But," gasped the astonished musician, "this is my room!"

"See here," said Ethelred, fiercely, "you can't fool me because I'm a newcomer. You just clear out of this room right smart, or it will be the worse for you!"

"You impudent fellow!" cried Mr. Hale, his anger growing as his courage rose, "if you don't get out of that bed at once, and leave this room with those clothes of yours, I'll cane you!" And he shook his dainty walking-stick at the occupant of his bed.

"You just come near enough," roared Ethelred, reaching down and recovering one of his shoes, "and I'll stave in your old head! You can't play any tricks on me."

At this point it occurred to Mr. Hale that he must be dealing with an escaped lunatic. He resolved to change his tactics.

"But, my dear sir," he urged, "that's my bed."

"You just get out of this room as quick as you can," returned Ethelred, "or I'll tell the professors on you!"

"What professors?"

"Professors Petersol and Salvini."

Mr. Hale was now convinced that he had to deal with a lunatic. There were no professors answering to such names in the college.

"Get out!" he roared, hoping to frighten the invader by the fierceness of his tones.

"Get out yourself, you idiot!" squawked Ethelred, at the top of his voice.

There had been a noise and pattering of footsteps outside during the foregoing dialogue. As Ethelred's voice ceased, there came a knock.

"Come in!" cried Mr. Hale, inwardly thankful that help had arrived.

The door opened, and the face of the brother infirmarian came into view.

"No you don't come in!" bawled Ethelred. "You're not going to work me. Get out of here both of you."

The brother now entered, and behind him, arrayed in their night-shirts and armed with sticks, shoes, pokers and one baseball bat, pattered six little barefoot boys. Their eyes were sticking out from curiosity.

The new arrivals were not long in appreciating the situation.

Mr. Hale, still standing behind his chair as though it were a rampart, was brandishing his cane. Ethelred, sitting up in bed, was holding a shoe, ready to throw at a moment's notice.

"There's a lunatic in that bed," explained the teacher of music.

"Lunatic, you old red-head!" retorted Ethelred; "I've got more sense than your whole family."

"Why," exclaimed one of the young gentlemen in white, "it's Ethelred Preston, his mama's darling!"

At this all the white-robed ones broke into a laugh, so hearty that one would find it hard to believe that they were the small boys of the Junior Division who, then and there, happened to be too ill to attend to regular work. It was Haines, temporarily indisposed by a headache, who recognized Ethelred. The five other boys, having been sick all that day, had not had the pleasure thus far of meeting the Darling. But Haines, during the two hours before bedtime, had told them enough of him to make this first moment of recognition a moment of ecstasy which they were not likely to forget.

"Come, sir," said the brother infirmarian; "get up out of that."

To the horror of the six little boys, Ethelred put his thumb to his nose and wriggled his fingers in scorn.

"I told you he was crazy!" said Mr. Hale.

"You people don't take *me* in!" said Ethelred. "Get out of this room! I wasn't born yesterday."

The brother was becoming angry.

"Get out, yourself, sir, or we shall have to have recourse to physical force!"

Before Ethelred could answer, another person arrived on the scene. It was Father Howard.

"Oh, here you are!" he said. "Why didn't you go to your dormitory? Your prefect reported you to me for being absent, and I've been looking for you since nine o'clock."

Ethelred became subdued at once.

"Professors Petersol and Salvini told me to come here."

If there was a twinkle in Father Howard's eye for a moment, let us trust that it was not recorded by the angel who keeps count and tally against disciplinarians.

"Go to your beds, boys," said Father Howard to the white-robed array.

They disappeared promptly, throwing wistful, lingering, longing looks over their shoulders.

"Now, sir, put on your clothes at once; and I'll take you to your dormitory. The professors you mention are not to be found in this college. You have been duped."

It was three months before Mr. Hale was able to see the joke in this little episode. Then he saw it and forgave the perpetrators. It was also one month before Professors Petersol and Salvini had fully squared accounts with Father Howard.

Chapter X

*IN WHICH EARL MERIWETHER RECEIVES ANOTHER
PUBLIC ADMONITION*

ON the following day, which was the last
Friday in January and the second day
in Ethelred Preston's career as a student in
Henryton College, the newcomer went about
more quietly. He had learned from his first
experiences that in entering upon college life
he was brought into relations with other
boys which were quite different from what
he had expected.

It had been his intention to borrow money
from everyone who was willing to lend, but
Devereux and Meriwether, by their remarks
on the previous afternoon, had caused him
to change his mind. His fellow students, satisfied with the preceding day's fun, were content, for the time being at least, to let him
alone. So the morning and afternoon wore
off without a break in the calm flow of college life.

During the recesses and recreations,
Ethelred clung to Earl. He was the only boy
in the college whom Ethelred cared about
consorting with.

"You see," he explained, as he gave Earl

a dig in the ribs, "we're both Protestants. I don't like these Catholics."

This remark fell upon Earl like a blow. It hurt his pride to feel that he should be put on the same footing with Preston. He knew, of course, that Preston was by no means a representative of the Protestant boy and that his Protestantism was rather a hatred of Catholics than any set form of worship. And yet this remark of Ethelred's galled him and awoke in him the old feeling of religious unrest.

"If you don't like these Catholics, so much the worse for you," answered Earl. "I know most of them here pretty well, and I can tell you that there are some fellows in this school who are leading lives as beautiful as the lives of the best people I ever read about in books."

"They're a lot of hypocrites," objected Ethelred.

"Oh, of course. In all the time that I've been attending school here, I never met a good-for-nothing fellow yet who didn't explain the conduct of those who acted decently on the ground of hypocrisy. That's a cheap way of showing jealousy or spite. I don't believe there are many hypocrites among boys—at least, little boys; and when you do come upon a hypocrite, you find him out pretty soon. But when you are thrown in with a boy day in day out for weeks and months, and notice that he will never do anything that he thinks is really wrong, it's nonsense to say that he's a hypocrite."

"Well," said Preston, "I haven't seen any of your pious boys around here. They don't seem to show any religion at all. Now there's that Devereux—you don't call *him* a pious boy!"

"Yes, but I do; there's not a better boy going. He was not remarkably good when he first came here from Philadelphia; but he changed inside of a month, and now he's next door to a saint."

"You're a fool," said the gentle Ethelred, in a croak. "That fellow pious! Why he laughs and jokes and skips around lively. Look at him now over there in that crowd. He's pushing and tugging and getting all the fun he can."

"I'm afraid you don't know much about piety, Ethelred."

"I guess I know a heap more about it than you do. I've been to camp meetings lots of times, and I've seen the pious people there. I've seen 'em on the platform and off it. They don't go about laughing and hopping and grinning. No, sir, you can jest bet yer boots. They look solemn and sad, and they talk that way, and they are just death on smoking and dancing and amoosements and jokes and card playing. You don't catch *them* playing jokes. Why, I can tell a pious feller as soon as I see him."

"So," said Earl, amused in spite of himself, "you don't think a person can be pious and cheerful at the same time."

"Not much."

"And," Earl continued, "if a man wants to be pious, according to your way of seeing it, he must not expect to enjoy himself, or have any fun at all."

"Why, that stands to reason; anybody who isn't a fool can see that," answered Ethelred.

"I thought you were an Episcopalian; *they* don't talk as you do."

"The old woman is—at least, she says so; but I'm not. I'm a Protestant, and I know what they believe mighty well."

"Well, you're wrong. The best class of Protestants agree with Catholics on that point. A person, according to them, is really pious when he does his duty and avoids sin through supernatural motives. Now, a boy can do his duty and avoid sin and at the same time have a jolly good time."

Ethelred snorted.

"If there's one thing I envy the Catholic boy," continued Earl, who was now talking on the subject which had lately absorbed his attention, "it is Confession."

"What!" squawked the Darling.

"It is beautiful to see the effect it has on them. They go into the confessional for a few moments and tell everything that is on their conscience to the priest. The priest sets them right if they need it, gives them good advice or encouragement when they are in trouble, and then gives them absolution. After that a boy feels that he has a new start."

"Have you ever read 'The Horrors of the Confeshing'?" asked Ethelred.

"I don't want to read it."

"It's good—it's full of lively things. Them priests ought all to be hanged. The idea of them fellows pretending they can forgive sins! And then their Mass! That's an invention of the devil. And what they call holy Com—"

"You'd better stop," broke in Earl, with a strange light in his eyes. "If there is one thing that has disgusted me with some people I have met, who call themselves Protestants, it is the indecent and exaggerated way in which they talk about Catholic practices.

Now take Communion. I've seen boys make their First Communion here twice, and I tell you it's the nicest sight I want to see. When those little boys go to Communion for the first time, some of them look like angels; and I'm sure if they were to die then, they would go straight to Heaven. If people who call themselves Protestants knew the good that Confession and Communion do to little boys, they wouldn't abuse these things, even if they did not believe in them."

But Ethelred was not easily to be silenced on the question of religion. As he admitted in the course of the conversation, he made no pretense of being a "professing Christian." At the same time, he had read and re-read all manner of books containing attacks on the Church, and he had, it would seem, attended the lectures of those highly delightful creatures, "reformed priests" and "escaped nuns." He was well armed, as he thought, for a vigorous onslaught on the Catholic Church and her ministers; and he poured into Earl's ears trite objections, stale slanders and silly stories till Earl was too angry to reply.

That afternoon in the classroom, Earl was more inattentive than ever. Some of Ethelred's objections to the Catholic Faith were new to him, and despite himself he kept turning them over in his mind. Yet, turn them as he might, no satisfactory answers suggested themselves. His hand was drumming idly upon the desk as his mind gave itself to these difficulties. The action of hand and brain were each involuntary.

"Five lines for drumming, Meriwether," said Mr. Gade.

Earl straightened up and bit his lip, while a shadow of annoyance passed over his face. The punishment was nothing extraordinary; there were several young gentlemen in the class given to beating the "Devil's tattoo" in season and out, in consequence of which Mr. Gade had been obliged to declare it unlawful with a penalty of five lines to be memorized for each offense. In calling out Earl, Mr. Gade had used his severest tones, instead of his usual matter-of-fact voice. It appeared to him that Earl was taking no pains to give satisfaction. This was the first time during the year that Earl had drummed upon his desk; and the teacher may be pardoned if, in the light of the preceding day's occurrence, he entertained a suspicion that the boy was trying to annoy him.

Earl was hurt. Why could not his teacher treat him as he treated the others?

"He's down on me" was his thought, and all the pride and vanity of his nature were again up in arms. Once these passions were awakened in our friend, they did not quickly subside. Slow to be aroused, he was slow to recover his usual equal mood. For the remainder of the hour, Earl sat motionless; but his blood was boiling. The fierce play of passion within his heart was something that terrified him. He left the classroom with his face set and hardened. All thought of religion, of goodness, all sweet and holy sentiments were gone. He retired to a deserted walk, where he paced up and down like a caged tiger.

At the end of class, Eddie Devereux remained at his desk, making a pretense of arranging his books and papers. When all had gone out, he approached Mr. Gade, blushing violently and very nervous.

"Mr. Gade, you wouldn't mind my saying something, sir?"

"Not at all, Eddie. I'm sure that you won't say anything very bad."

"It's about Earl, sir."

"Well, what about him?" At the mention of Earl's name the smile of encouragement disappeared from the teacher's face.

"I think, sir, he was trying to pay attention the day you sent him from the room."

"It didn't look that way, Eddie. I'm afraid that you are prejudiced."

"I'm his friend," said loyal Ed, simply, "and I know," he went on, "that Earl is a good boy. I think that he did more for me than any boy here when I first came. He gave me a little talking once because I wasn't behaving in chapel, and it made me so ashamed of myself that it was worth more to me than a dozen sermons. Please don't think hard of Earl, Mr. Gade. He's troubled about something; I'm sure he wasn't thinking of what he was doing when he was drumming this afternoon."

Mr. Gade was secretly delighted with Ed's loyalty to his friend. At the same time, he was decidedly of the opinion that Ed was mistaken in his estimate of Earl's conduct. As the reader knows, it was Mr. Gade who misjudged. It must be said in his defense, however, that, owing to Earl's extreme reticence, he had nothing to judge from but the appearance of things. Ed, on the other hand, having heard Earl's story, was sufficiently aware of his friend's struggles and troubles to be thoroughly convinced of his good faith. Yet, knowing them in confidence, he did not feel at liberty to reveal to Mr. Gade any of the details which Earl had revealed to him.

Hence the interview failed to produce the effect which Ed had hoped for. He went away then, feeling that his offices as mediator had utterly failed. On dismissing Devereux with a few kind words, Mr. Gade, leaving the classroom, took his way across the yard to the junior students' library.

He was within a few feet of the library door when he unexpectedly came upon Earl, still pacing up and down the lonely walk. Earl was advancing toward him the meeting was inevitable. At first Mr. Gade was in a state of irresolution about saluting Earl kindly. There was a stony, repellent stare in the boy's eyes as he drew nearer. Would it not be better to pass the troublesome pupil with a cold recognition? Any friendly overture made to Earl in his present exasperated and sullen state of mind would lay the teacher open to a slight. Besides, Earl was the inferior; he should be shown that his present course deserved rebuke.

On the other hand, perhaps Eddie Devereux was right; or, again, if not altogether right, perhaps there was some truth in his defense of his friend. Moreover—and this was the most important point—a little kindness rarely goes amiss. Mr. Gade resolved, though it cost him a struggle, to try kindness.

"Good afternoon, Earl," he said with a smile and in gentle tones.

"Good afternoon," said Earl in surly tones, touching his cap gingerly and walking on. Earl's manner was harsh and repellent. Mr. Gade's courtesy was indeed a courtesy ill returned.

"I'm afraid that Eddie is wholly wrong," reflected the teacher, sadly, as he walked on, "and my attempt at kindness has gone for nothing."

Mr. Gade's "attempt at kindness" may have gone for nothing according to the world's measurement; but according to a higher and holier measurement, it had gone for much.

In answering thus uncourteously Mr. Gade's kind salutation, Earl had acted on the ugly spur of the moment and without fully realizing what he was doing. It was only when he had turned his back upon his teacher that a fuller sense of his conduct came upon him. Clear and distinct from the black background of his passion shone the kind eyes which had looked into his momentarily with such sympathy; clear and distinct from the black background of his passion the teacher's thin, delicate face, worn with sickness, haunted him, and as that kind face fastened upon his imagination, the clouds of passion thinned and scattered. How unpardonably rude he had been! He had been boorish; he had returned kindness with bitterness. The tears came to Earl's eyes. A chance had been given him to return to the former footing with his teacher, even to explain everything, and he had thrown it away.

Earl was thoroughly humbled. He had been convinced, a moment before, that he was a persecuted boy. Now he began to entertain doubts. If he could but apologize. Alas! He had let his chance escape. The same pride which had led him to act thus discourteously, now, under another shape, stood between him and the making of a full submission. But in his heart there arose a short, earnest prayer to God for grace and light and strength. So Mr. Gade's salutation, though it had brought him a slight, was not without fruit; and Eddie's mediation had not been vain. It has been well said that for every act of kindness performed in this world of ours, there is one sin the less.

Chapter XI

*IN WHICH ETHELRED TAKES MORE ROPE THAN
DEVEREUX HAD COUNTED UPON*

"WELL, here's the rope," whispered Ed
Devereux, stooping and raising a
large coil from beside the trunk of the tree
near the eastern wall. "Just keep quiet a
minute while I tie an end to this tree."

It was a dark night. The cold had grown
more intense during the past twenty-four
hours, and the wind which came whistling
through the trees set the teeth of the four
chattering.

"Are you sure that rope will reach all the
way down?" asked Ethelred.

"Sure and certain, with ten or twelve feet
to spare. There now, the rope is tied safe."

"There's a light down there in the street,"
objected Ethelred, peering over the wall.

"Of course there is," said Haines, who was
standing beside him. "That street is a part
of the town, even if it is deserted; and the
light comes from an old-style lamp-post half
a block away."

"You had better go," urged Earl. "The bell
for the end of recess will ring in a few minutes, and it's no use standing here and

freezing to death."

Ethelred gazed down again. Despite the glimmer from the lamp-post, it looked very black and mysterious beneath. He regretted that he had determined to descend by a rope.

"Look here. Maybe that rope isn't sound; it might break."

"If it does," said Eddie, "we'll give it to you for nothing."

"I don't care about risking my neck. Say, Eddie Devereux, would you mind climbing down just to see how it goes?"

"Next thing you'll want me to run away for you. If you don't hurry, your hands will be so cold and numb that you won't be able to use them. Go on yourself, or give up; we can't stay here much longer."

"I don't know what to do," whined Ethelred.

"Very well, Darling," said Eddie, coolly, "then I'll unfasten this rope, and we'll all go to prayers." And Eddie made for the tree.

"No, no; I'll go. Good-bye, everybody."

The three took a strong hold on the rope; Ethelred mounted the wall with no little trepidation, caught the coil, dropped over— then all was silence, save for the labored breathing of the three boys above and the noise of shoes scraping and knocking against the stone wall.

A minute passed before they heard Ethelred's whistle—the agreed signal that all was well. On pulling up the rope, they found that it lacked about twenty feet of its former length.

Ethelred had taken it away as a souvenir.

"Well, that's what I call mean!" exclaimed Eddie.

"We're well rid of such a boy," commented Earl. "He has no sense of decency."

Roger Haines was chuckling.

"It's one on you, Eddie," he said at length. "You might have sent the boy off by the back way, but you *would* have this romantic climbing down by a rope. The joke's on you. That rope belongs to the gymnasium, and you'll have to pay the damages."

"I don't mind the expense," said the rueful Eddie, "but it's getting found out that bothers me. I'll lose my privileges for good conduct, although my conduct has been perfectly proper. In assisting Ethelred to leave, I consider myself as a benefactor to the college."

"Yes, he's a good riddance," said Roger. "But there goes the bell. Good night, boys, I'm going to take a run; my ears and toes and hands are beginning to freeze."

In the dormitory, the prefect, shortly after night prayers, noticed the absence of Ethelred, and he darted an inquiring look in Earl's direction. Earl, in common with the majority of the students, was on his knees.

Two or three minutes later, when he had arisen, the prefect came over.

"Earl, do you know anything about Ethelred Preston?"

"Yes, sir."

"Where is he?"

"By this time, sir, he ought to be on board the cars for home. There's the engine whistling now. He's run away, sir, and I helped him."

The prefect shrugged his shoulders and returned to his place.

"That's the end of Ethelred Preston so far as we are concerned," he thought.

But he was greatly mistaken.

Once Ethelred touched the ground, he was himself again, which he immediately proved by cutting off as much of the rope as he could reach. Hurriedly coiling this about his arm, and wondering what he should do with it, he walked smartly down the street in the direction of the depot.

And now Ethelred began to repent him of his new acquisition. He had taken the rope instinctively; but what was he to do with it? To throw it away would be wasteful. If he could but trade it off, were it only for a collar button!

Thus lamenting, Ethelred reached the station.

"Evening paper, sir, the *Star!*" cried a tiny youngster whose face was hidden by a tremendous "comforter."

A bright idea struck Ethelred.

"See here, Johnnie, how many papers will you give me for this rope? It's a splendid rope and worth at least forty cents."

"I don't want a rope."

"You could hang a man with this," urged Ethelred, "and the rope would be as good as new. Hold on, don't go away. What evening papers have you got?"

"The *Star* and the *Post*."

"And how much are they?"

"*Star*, three cents; *Post*, two."

"Take the whole rope for five cents; give me a *Star* and a *Post*, and we'll call it a bargain. It's a splendid rope."

"All right, sir; I'll trade."

"Couldn't you throw in an extra *Star*?"

"You said one."

"Come, throw in one more copy," he pleaded.

Eventually Ethelred entered the station with three evening papers. He paid seventy cents for a second class ticket and, having twelve minutes to wait, seated himself and took up the evening *Star*.

He had been reading for several minutes, when he suddenly gave a low whistle. With mouth agape and protruding eyes, he read and reread a certain news item of about thirty lines.

"This beats Jericho!" he exclaimed, and dropping the paper, he fell into a study.

An hour later that night, a card was handed Father Edmunds. He glanced at it.

"What!" he said. "I thought that chapter was closed."

And he threw the card on his table and hastened to the parlor.

It read:

> Master Ethelred Preston,
> Albany Villa, Brighton
> [At Home Tuesdays]

Chapter XII

*IN WHICH ETHELRED "GETS RELIGION" AND
TURNS OVER A NEW LEAF*

"WELL, sir, what do you want now?"
Ethelred was standing in the dimly
lighted parlor, fumbling his hat.

"I've come back," answered Ethelred.

The president turned up the light and
fixed a stern glance upon the runaway, who
lowered his eyes and gave very evident signs
of extreme nervousness.

"Come back for what, Master Preston?"

"I'm sorry I run away."

"Yes, but running away here subjects the
offender to expulsion."

"But I only went as far as the depot. Then
I began to think. It would bust my mother's
heart if she knew that her boy had run away
and been expelled."

The president was puzzled. The runaway
before him had the appearance of a worthless boy. The reports concerning him from
prefects and teachers were to the effect that
he was as worthless as he seemed to be.
But how to square all this with the letter
from his mother, the testimonials from the
Mayor of Brighton and from the pastor of

the Episcopalian church?

"It was because I didn't think, sir, that I run away. I got red hot when the old—when my mother sent me here, and I made up my mind to be as ugly as I could. But I got religion down at the depot. If you let me come back, I'll turn a new leaf. You don't catch me monkeying anymore."

These words of Ethelred, vulgarly couched though they were, satisfied several of the president's difficulties. Had not Mrs. Preston stated that her son was likely to act first and think afterwards—to take the leap and then look? Had not the Mayor of Brighton warned him that the boy meditated running away? The bad points to be looked for in the boy's character had been verified. Was there not a reasonable hope, especially in view of Ethelred's confession, that the good ones were now to come into evidence? The president felt that he was at length beginning to understand the strange character before him.

"Well, Ethelred, I will give you one more chance to redeem yourself. I now receive you, but conditionally. To be frank, despite the high character your parents enjoy, you do not seem to be at all up to the standard which we require of our students. Your ways and manners and views are such as we find in those whose associations are of the very lowest."

"I used to go with our coachman all the time," said Ethelred, looking gratified.

"Indeed. Well, you must mend your manners without delay. You have already given offense to the boys here by your profanity. If I hear anything of the sort again, you shall go at once."

"I'll stop sure; I only talked that way to show off."

"What a high ideal! As though cursing were an accomplishment. Now, I shall write you a note of admission to the dormitory. Go there at once, and remember that you are here on probation—on trial. Were not your mother on the way to Europe, I doubt whether I should receive you at all."

*   *   *   *   *

"I say, how in the world did you get back?" asked Eddie Devereux early the next morning, catching Ethelred's arm as the two came out of the washroom.

"I walked back," was the smart answer. "I told you fellows I was going to fool you a little bit before I left."

"And do you mean to say that you got up

that plan of running away just for the sake of fooling me and Earl Meriwether?"

"That's just about the size of it."

"And what did you do with that piece of rope? You cut off about twenty feet of it. I want it back."

"That was a part of the joke too. You needn't get mad; you fellows had your fun out of me, and now I'm getting even with you. You can't fool this chicken."

Ed's vanity was hurt more than he liked to confess even to himself. He was a quick-witted youngster and knew it. To be thus taken in by a "greenhorn" was a real subject of mortification to him. He began to suspect that there was in the newcomer more than he had given him credit for.

"You may remember, Darling, that I lent you seventy-five cents to help you run away."

"Maybe I do, and maybe I don't."

"And I said you might keep it, provided you did not come back to college."

"That so?"

"Now you're back, and I'll be glad to get that money."

"What—all of it?"

"Certainly."

"Will you let me off if I pay you twenty cents?"

"Not much."

"It's thirty cents on the dollar."

"I want that money—every cent of it. Come on, Preston."

Preston looked concerned for a moment; suddenly his face brightened.

"Look here, Devereux; that money was a part of the joke!"

"Suppose it was?"

"Well, just this—I'm not going to spoil the joke; it's too good. I'd like to pay you, but I can't."

"Your jokes are pretty expensive ones, Darling. No, sir; you just pay me back that money."

"I wouldn't spoil such a joke for twice the amount!" protested Ethelred, who was now speaking with extreme animation.

"Do you mean to say that you don't intend to return me my money?"

Ethelred's face grew troubled, and he took a moment's thought. Suddenly his face brightened, and he said, with no attempt to conceal an expression of triumph:

"I'll pay it if the president allows the debt."

There was no doubt that Ethelred possessed a large store of low cunning. He had outwitted Devereux, but he had outwitted him on grounds with which Ed—to his credit, be it said—was utterly unfamiliar.

With a hoarse laugh and slapping his hand over his vest pocket, Ethelred walked off, leaving Devereux quite vexed. But the little lad's sense of humor soon came to his rescue. Aside from the incidental meanness, the joke was not bad. Besides, turn about is fair play. Ethelred had made him a return in kind; and as for the money, Ed resolved to let the claim go. He also resolved to keep a sharp eye on the borrower.

Before morning prayers, accordingly, he summoned Earl and Roger and told them of his interview with the Darling.

"He's got the joke on us," said Earl, "and I suppose I'm out fifty or sixty cents too."

"There's something strange about the whole affair," mused Roger. "It may be that he plotted this trick on us; but if he did, then he is a magnificent actor. Somehow, I can't bring myself to believe that he had no intention of running away last night."

"As for me," said Eddie frankly, "I don't want to believe it. It's terrible to think I've been made a fool of by a chap like that, but it looks pretty clear against us. If he were to tell his story to the boys in the yard, I don't think there's a fellow who wouldn't believe it. I wonder how he got back and how he accounted for his absence."

"I lay awake till ten o'clock," said Earl, "and he didn't come to the dormitory up to that time. The first I saw of him was this morning, when he jumped out of bed looking jollier than he has looked since he came here."

"Ethelred Preston is a conundrum," said Eddie, "and he needs study. It seems to me that he ought not to be in this college at all."

"Me too," assented Haines. "In the meantime, we can wait till we learn more."

"Yes," added Earl, "and in the meantime, too, it wouldn't be bad to suspend judgment."

"That's just what I'm doing," returned Devereux. "I'm suspending judgment as hard as I can. By the way, Earl, what did the prefect ask you in the dormitory last night?"

"He asked me whether I knew anything about Preston's whereabouts, and I told him that Preston had run away and that he was just about going off in the train which we heard whistling while he was speaking to me."

"Did Mr. Raymond suspect that you had anything to do with his running away?"

"He didn't ask me whether I had anything to do with it," responded Earl, in a manner so reticent that Ed resolved at once to probe further.

"But didn't you tell him something?"

"Not about you, Ed or Haines."

"There! It's just what I expected," cried Ed, triumphantly. "You've told on yourself—now, haven't you?"

"The fact is," returned Earl, with blushing uneasiness, "I simply said I had helped Ethelred off."

"What an elegant clam you would make, Earl. It is as hard to get information out of you sometimes as sense out of a clothesline. I see your little plan. You want to take all the blame on yourself and save me."

"Me too," added Roger.

"Oh, you had nothing particular to do with it, Roger. You played a quiet second fiddle. But if it had not been for me, Earl wouldn't have let Ethelred go at all! If anyone is to blame, it is I."

"Not at all," said Earl; "I started him with the idea, and it seems to me that I am the responsible one. And even supposing you hadn't as much to do with it as I had, Ed, still I didn't say that I was alone in the matter; I simply said that I had helped. I'm on the blacklist anyhow just at present, and a little thing like that won't change my position one way or the other."

At the beginning of morning studies, the vice president entered the junior students' study hall and made a few remarks upon Ethelred's running away and subsequent repentance. He informed the boys that Ethelred, owing to a peculiar combination of circumstances, had been allowed to return, but on probation. He concluded thus:

"I am sorry to say that one of the leading boys of the Junior Division has actually abetted the newcomer in his foolish notion. As the one who assisted him has confessed on himself, I shall take no action; but I cannot refrain from expressing my regret publicly that he should thus lend his countenance to conduct which is far worse than any ordinary breach of discipline. The boy who helps another to run away from school assumes a serious responsibility."

Earl hung his head, and his face was suffused with blushes. It was the third public reprehension of his college course, and they had all three fallen within forty-eight hours of each other. Eddie Devereux was hardly less concerned. He knew that, through an act of friendship, Earl had laid himself open to this public rebuke.

Before class, Eddie was at the Prefect of Discipline's room.

"You were talking about Earl this morning, Father, when you spoke of the leading boy that had helped the Darling—I mean Ethelred—to run away."

"That is true, Ed; what about it?"

"But he wasn't to blame, Father. It was my fault. Earl had a scruple because the first time he met Ethelred he had made a remark against the college. He thought this remark was the cause of Ethelred's wanting to run away; but I settled the scruple for him. I said that it would be a good thing for the college if Ethelred were to get out. He's a queer sort of a fellow, and does not seem to fit in here. So I persuaded Earl to let him go, and it was I, Father, that engineered the whole thing. Of course, Earl helped, but I was the leader, and Earl was simply following my plans. Last night Earl told the prefect that he helped Ethelred off just in order to get me out of trouble."

"I am pleased to hear your side of the story, Eddie; but how could you bring yourself to help a boy run away? You know that is a serious matter."

Devereux then explained his reasons for taking this action, much in the same way as he had set them forth before Earl. While secretly amused, Father Howard was pleased by the explanation. Whatever he might think of the reasoning, he felt sure, at all events, that Earl and Ed had acted with some regard to the promptings of their consciences.

"Thank you for speaking to me about this," said Father Howard when Ed had come to an end. "It relieves me very much to know that in helping Ethelred off there was nothing of the weakness and human respect and disregard for consciences which one naturally expects in such things. I no longer look upon Earl's action in the same way; and I wish you would tell Earl so. As for yourself, I forgive you too; only, please don't help runaways anymore.

"And now," continued Father Howard, "I have a word to say about Ethelred Preston. From what you have said, I gather that yourself and Earl and many of the boys do not look upon him as a fit student for Henryton College. There were reasons for your thinking so yesterday. But it is well to know that Ethelred came here in a state of rebellion; he was not himself from the time of his entrance till he ran away. On reaching the railroad station last night, it seems that he entered into himself. Then, of his own free will, he came back here, and after apologizing for his previous conduct, he made very satisfactory promises to the president of the college. Now I ask you, and you, in turn, will ask Earl and others of the boys to give the newcomer another chance. Don't condemn him prematurely. Show him a little kindness if you can."

"All right, sir," answered Eddie. "We'll give him a fair chance."

"And, Eddie, kindly send Earl here; I wish to smooth over as much as possible the little misunderstanding of this morning."

"All right, Father; I thank you very much."

As Devereux left the room, he wore a broad grin. First, he had vindicated Earl; secondly, it struck him as a fit theme for smiling that the boy who had made such satisfactory promises of behavior before going to bed should begin the new day by lying and by repudiating his honest debts.

"So he did run away after all. I wonder what brought him back. Maybe he came back because he entered into himself, but it's pretty hard for me to believe that. I'd give a dollar to know the real reason why he came back."

And if Eddie had known the real reason for Ethelred's return, this story would be finished in very short order indeed.

Chapter XIII

IN WHICH ETHELRED BECOMES MORE MYSTERIOUS AND EARL MORE HEROIC

EDDIE DEVEREUX, notwithstanding his doubts concerning the sincerity of Ethelred's purpose of amendment, put himself, with the best of will, to carrying out the behest of Father Howard. He told such of his school fellows as he came upon that Ethelred was really going to turn over a new leaf and pleaded with them to give the interesting newcomer another chance. Thus appealed to, the junior students made no difficulty in laying aside their prejudices and feelings against Ethelred. For the present, at least, he might go his way unmolested. Indeed, they were almost deferential to him in their eagerness to comply with Father Howard's wishes.

Among themselves, however, there were many jokes passed about Ethelred's manner of escape from the college. These witticisms were not intended for Ethelred's ears; but that artless youth, Peter Lane, out of sheer benevolence, thought fit to make them known to him.

"I say," he said, seating himself beside

Ethelred, who was watching a game of handball—"I say, Darling, the fellows have been telling me that you're going to drop your nonsense and turn over a new leaf."

"Is that any of your business?"

"Well, you see, I'm not going to tease you anymore," explained the diminutive youth, rising and standing with his arms akimbo before Ethelred, "and I thought maybe you'd like to know it."

Ethelred glared savagely at the amiable urchin, but said nothing.

"You were mad at me yesterday, I know," continued Pete, "and you started roughhouse on me when you got me alone. It would have been awful roughhouse for me, if Earl Meriwether hadn't come in and started roughhouse on you. But I just want to tell you I am not mad about it in the least."

"Confound it!" growled Ethelred, "who cares whether you're mad or not?"

"But you ought to care. You see, I'm in with the other fellows, and we're going to give you a fair chance."

"Do you think, you wretched little sardine, that I care a snap whether *you* give me a chance or not?"

"You ought to, Darling."

"But I don't."

"That's because you're so green," said Peter complacently and not one whit abashed. "Say,"—here Peter broke into melodious giggles—"you ought to hear some of the jokes that the fellows have been getting off on you."

"What jokes?" asked Ethelred, raising his head and speaking with an animation which had not, thus far, characterized his share of the dialogue.

"Oh, any amount—about your running away, you know. Some say you ran away just because you got too much rope."

Peter laughed full-throated, while Ethelred gazed at him stolidly.

"Others," Peter continued, "say you didn't get rope enough, and that's the reason you went off with twenty feet that belonged to the gymnasium."

Ethelred's stolid face changed at these words to an expression of anger, while Peter broke into another ringing laugh.

"And one of the fellows says that you took enough rope to hang yourself with easily; but you were afraid to hang yourself for fear of spoiling the rope."

"Get away from here, will you, or I'll kick you all over the yard!" cried Ethelred.

"Oh!—very well," said Peter, and he added

with much dignity as he turned upon his heel, "I guess I know how to take a hint."

"Halloa Preston!" called Earl from across the yard. "Your trunk has just come. If you like I'll take you over to the clothes room."

At this bit of news Ethelred involuntarily gave a start; but, recovering himself so quickly that those about failed to notice it, he arose and followed Earl.

"By the way, Ethelred," said Earl kindly, as the two were walking toward the clothes room, "if there's any little thing I can do for you, just let me know. I might help you out in some of your lessons, as you're a little behind the class in the matter they saw before you came, or give you a few hints one way or the other. It's a little hard on a newcomer here in the beginning because he is a stranger and often doesn't know the ways of boarding schools."

"I guess I can look out for myself right smart now," responded the grateful youth. "I got caught yesterday, but you can bet I don't get caught again."

"I suppose not," assented Earl. "If you settle down to study in earnest, it is not likely that the boys will try to bother you again. All you've got to do is to keep quiet for a week or so, till the boys begin to know you and you feel more at home. They are good fellows here, but some of them like to tease. Now, by keeping quiet for a while, you keep these fellows who like to tease from getting a handle on you, and—"

"You needn't preach," interrupted the Darling in his fascinating croak.

Earl colored.

"Oh!" he ejaculated, as he bit his lip.

"Here's the clothes room—come right in; there's your trunk."

If there ever was a trunk that merited the epithet "dainty," it was the trunk of Ethelred Preston.

It was small, with bands, apparently of silver, which were fastened by numerous buttons of a golden color. Above the lock was a silver plate with the monogram E. P. traced in lines of a rare delicacy. It was such a trunk as the most callous baggage man would instinctively "handle with care."

Ethelred fell to rummaging in his pockets. Out of one he took a handful of buttons, a spool of thread, a cork in which were stuck four or five needles of various sizes, and a large clasp knife. Out of another, a piece of bees-wax, a magnet, a can-opener, a small ball of twine and a bunch of keys, which he examined carefully.

"Halloa!" he exclaimed.

"What's the matter, Ethelred?"

"I—I've lost my trunk key. It was on this bunch when I came; but it's gone. I've been robbed!"

"There are no thieves in this school," said Earl, sharply. He added in a milder tone, as he stooped to examine the lock of the trunk, "It's too bad. I see that it's a skeleton key, too, and I'm afraid the brother has nothing to open it with. I say, Brother John, Ethelred Preston has lost the key of his trunk. Do you think you can open it for him, please?"

The brother, laying aside some work upon the long table which ran almost the length of the room, stepped over and scrutinized the lock. Neither Earl nor Brother John, so absorbed were they in examining the trunk, noticed how pale Ethelred had become.

"I think there will be some difficulty in opening this trunk," said the clothes keeper; "the lock is not an ordinary one."

Ethelred drew a deep breath.

"You needn't take no trouble," he said in his usual choice diction; "there's another key at home, and I can send for it, and get it inside of three days. While I'm waiting I reckon Meriwether can lend me some of his duds just as I need 'em."

Ethelred, as his last remark shows, was himself again.

"All right, Ethelred," said Earl, heroically. He was forcing himself to remember, poor boy, that Ethelred's mother and his own had been dear friends, and it consoled him to think that his mother, now in Heaven, must surely know and appreciate the struggles against feeling and sentiment which he was making for love of her.

"Lend me a few collars, then, and some cuffs, and a tie or two, and five or six collar buttons."

In a word, before they left the clothes room, Ethelred had secured the loan of a suit of clothes, a pair of suspenders, of earmuffs, and of gloves, a scarf, a silk handkerchief and a football sweater. The boy had a passion for borrowing.

During study hours that day, Ethelred was observed to be writing a great deal; and in the intervals for play and the recesses, he was seen to hold several interviews with a certain day scholar, Farwell by name, whose reputation with the boarders at Henryton stood by no means high.

"I'm afraid," remarked Devereux to Earl, shortly before supper, "that the Darling is up to some new mischief. Somehow, I can't help keeping my eyes on him. You may be sure he wasn't talking to that day scholar for nothing. I'm not quite certain yet, but I'm willing to bet that he gave him a letter, perhaps two or three letters, to post outside."

"Perhaps he doesn't know the rule," suggested Earl, charitably.

"Oh, no—of course not," returned Eddie, with a touch of sarcasm in his voice. "And then, too, I've noticed that he fights shy of most of the boarders except you."

"I've noticed that too," said Earl, with a smile. "In fact, he's been good enough to call my attention to it. He says he likes to talk to me because I'm not a Catholic like the rest of the fellows. After dinner, he stuck to me the whole time and abused everything Catholic. Oh, it was hard! He's got the idea into his head that I am being hoodwinked by the people here, and so he's trying to put the Catholic Church before me as he sees it. To him it's a nightmare." Earl paused a moment with a vexed expression upon his face, and added: "If he only knew the effect that his talk is having on me, I think he would leave the Catholic Church severely alone."

This last remark Eddie connected with an

incident which happened after supper. It was Saturday, and, though not the regular monthly Confession day, a goodly number of the junior students, many of whom were weekly communicants, repaired to the chapel. Among those stationed near Father Noland's confessional, Eddie started on perceiving Earl Meriwether. One by one, in regular order, the boys entered the confessional and, returning shortly, stationed themselves further back in the chapel, where, after the manner of well-trained Catholic youths, they renewed their good resolutions and begged for strength to observe them. Eddie was one of the first to make his Confession and, on finishing, took a place where he could keep his eye on Earl. You may be sure, the warm-hearted lad prayed fervently for his friend.

Ten or twelve minutes passed. All the penitents of Father Noland had had their turn except Earl, who still knelt motionless, his eyes fixed on the beautiful statue of the Sacred Heart.

"I wonder whether he is really going in," mused Eddie, and he prayed again and again that it might be so.

His eyes brightened when Earl, a few moments later, with downcast eyes and clasped hands, entered the confessional. He came out so soon, however, as to surprise Eddie; and as he walked from the confessional back into the body of the chapel, he gave his waiting friend a quick glance. Eddie read the meaning of that glance. It meant: "Wait for me; I have something to tell you."

A few minutes passed in silent prayer; then the two arose, genuflected and went out together.

"Eddie," Earl began, as they made their way down the stairs, "you think I went to Confession, don't you? Well, I didn't go that far exactly. Here's what I did. I went in to Father Noland and told him that I was a Protestant—you see, he didn't look at me, nor seem to know who I was—and I said that I didn't care about making a Confession, but that I felt troubled a great deal and would like to have a talk with him in private."

"And do you mean to say," broke in Eddie, "that you've had your talk and told all your troubles already?"

"Indeed, I do not," answered Earl with a faint smile. "I told him a little; that is, I gave him a general idea of the things that were bothering me; and he proposed that I should go to his room and talk the whole matter over with him at greater length. I'm going; but honestly, Eddie, I'm awfully upset just at present. Things have come to such a pass that I have been almost forced to go and consult with somebody."

"It must be pretty bad with you, Earl," said Eddie, with much sympathy in his voice, "or you would keep your troubles to yourself. I've noticed all along that you don't talk overmuch about your own doings and feelings."

"No," assented Earl, "I've always made it a point to keep myself to myself; and, if anything, I have carried it too far. But now I'm going to try and open my heart for once. And I hope you'll pray for me, Eddie, for I feel that there's something serious about the present state of affairs—that is, I think that I've come to a point where I have to change in one way or another, and that change is to be for better or for worse. It's the jumping off place."

"You may rely on it, I'll pray for you, Earl. And don't worry, you'll have no trouble in talking to Father Noland. He has been dealing with boys all his life, and nothing you can tell him will astonish him in the least."

"I believe you, Eddie, and besides he's so old. His long white hair and his kind face and his pleasant voice give him such a fatherly air. Even in the few minutes I spent with him just now, I found that he is even kinder than he looks, which is saying a great deal. I'm going to Father Howard now to get permission to see Father Noland in his room during first hour of studies."

Despite these words, it was with no little nervousness and hesitation that Earl, ten minutes later, knocked at Father Noland's door.

Chapter XIV

*IN WHICH EARL HAS A MOMENTOUS INTERVIEW
WITH FATHER NOLAND*

"TAKE a chair, Earl," said Father Noland, laying aside his glasses and breviary and pointing to a seat beside him. "You are welcome, my boy."

Father Noland had risen to greet his visitor. He seated himself after these words, but the act of courtesy was not lost upon the boy. Earl was extremely sensitive to kindness and consideration.

"Thank you, Father," answered Earl, as he

took the chair which the venerable priest had motioned him to. "I hate to come to any man with my troubles."

The Father smiled.

"And I believe I understand your reason," he said. "You are one of those characters that are called self-reliant. You want to fight out everything by yourself."

"I believe so, Father."

"With you, Earl, it is a good trait carried, perhaps, to extremes; and extremes are bad. It is well sometimes for the wisest of us to take counsel. As the saying is—a saying, of course, that is not true in many cases—'no man is a good judge in his own cause.'"

"Yes, Father; I am beginning to find that out. I am very proud, and it hurts me to talk of my troubles. But I am going to talk about them now, and to begin with I should like to speak of my troubles with Mr. Gade."

Earl then proceeded to narrate the untoward events which had lately come to pass in the classroom. He did not give Mr. Gade's side, for the simple reason that he was ignorant of it. Moreover, with the narrowness of judgment which years and experience alone can remove, Earl did not even imagine that there was any other side, any other standpoint than his own. But the venerable Father, who lent him an attentive and sympathetic ear, could easily read between the lines and supply the omissions of an honest, though one-sided, statement.

"Well, Earl," he said, "is it owing to these classroom troubles alone that you have come to see me?"

"No, sir; there's something far more serious besides. It is the question of religion. I am a Lutheran, Father, and I feel bound by a promise which I made to my mother to hold fast to my religion. But then, on the other hand, my conscience is worrying me a great deal and insists that I must become a Catholic. Just three days ago, I made up my mind for good—at least, so I thought then—never even to think of joining the Catholic Church. Up to that time, I had been doubting, and didn't know my own mind. I did not feel quite sure at that time that it was my duty to become a Catholic; I only doubted. But since then every doubt I had as to my duty to join the Catholic Church has been removed; and now the one thing that holds me back is the promise which I made to my mother when she was on her deathbed."

"Just a moment ago, Earl, you said that you had made up your mind never again to consider the claims of the Catholic Church."

"Yes, Father—three days ago."

"How comes it, then, that you have so suddenly changed your resolution?"

"Father, I have been converted, or rather next to converted, by somebody else."

"By Eddie Devereux, perhaps?"

"No, Father, but by our newcomer—by Ethelred Preston."

"Indeed!" exclaimed Father Noland, opening his eyes. "Why, I was under the impression that Ethelred is not a Catholic. In fact, he told me so himself in very emphatic language."

"He is not a Catholic, Father. He is what most people call a Protestant, though he is no more a Protestant, as I understand religion, than I am a Jew. A real Protestant is entitled to respect; but these fellows whose only religious practices consist in ridiculing and abusing and lying about Catholics, and in telling bug-a-boo stories of priests and nuns and the Inquisition, have no right whatever to be called Protestants. They are—they are—" Earl paused for a moment. "They are either great fools or silly liars. Now I think Ethelred is a fool."

"But how in the name of common sense did a boy whom you consider a fool convert you, Earl?"

"In two ways, sir. First of all, Ethelred's conduct and manners forced me to think of what I might have been if I had not been sent to school here. Ever since I've been at Henryton, Father, I've had a chance to go with the nicest and best boys one would want to meet with. I don't mean to say that I have not come across any bad boys; they have come here, sir, and most of them of that kind have either changed or gone. At any rate, where there are so many good fellows to choose from, there's no need to go with bad boys. So, it was easy for me in a way to be good here until lately, and then I began to see that something else was necessary besides good company. I have to fight against myself, too; and it is a terrible fight sometimes! For nearly the last six or seven months, my temptations have been teaching me the meaning of that Scripture text, 'the kingdom of heaven is taken by violence.' I used to wonder what it meant. But now I find it harder and harder to be good, and it seems to me that if I were to begin to go wrong, I might become very bad."

"So you have found it out at last," put in Father Noland. "My dear Earl, I have been watching your course with interest ever since you came here, and I have long thought that you would some day come to see me, just as you have come today; and it has long been my intention to tell you, on your coming, my opinion that you are going to turn out, in all probability, either a very bad, or a very good man. Yes, Earl; I firmly believe that for you there is no middle course. Earl, you are a boy of very strong passions."

Earl gazed in astonishment at Father Noland.

"Who told you that, sir?"

Father Noland laughed softly.

"When an everyday man brings a watch to the watchmaker, and while he is telling what he knows about it, the watchmaker at a single glance into the works knows all that the man can tell, and sometimes a great deal more. You take the allegory?"

"Yes, Father; but I didn't think anyone knew what you said about me except God. In fact, I didn't know it myself till lately. Now with regard to Ethelred Preston, Father; what I say is not to be used against him."

"Of course not, Earl. I feel bound to secrecy on everything that takes place between us in this talk."

"I don't like to say it, for I hate to say anything against any boy, but I can't keep it back if I wish to make myself clear to you. It is this: Ethelred Preston is a bad boy. I don't mean to say that he is rude and rough and uncouth; anyone here can see for himself, without being told of it, that Ethelred is not a gentleman. How he came to get such manners is beyond me, for his mother is a lady. But besides being rude and boorish, he is a bad boy. He says wicked and vile things. He has no sense of honesty. He goes by his feelings and doesn't seem to know the meaning of self-restraint. And as I got to noticing this, I began to think of what might happen to me. I wasn't afraid, Father, of becoming rude and boorish; I don't think that I could ever fall so low, with my mother's memory and my college training upon me, as to lose all sense of decency. But, then, it did seem to me that I might fall very soon into sinful ways, and that if once I went that way, I might lose control over myself. And then, although I should not resemble Ethelred in his manners, still I should be like him in his badness of heart. I don't know, Father, whether I make my feelings clear to you."

"I understand, Earl; you have gone below the surface of things where people of the world generally stay, and you are trying to look at your position from God's standpoint.

God does not look at the manners of a man so much as at his heart. He judges boors and gentlemen from their interior dispositions. Sinlessness and culture do not necessarily go hand in hand."

"Yes, Father; that's it. It seemed to me that if I were once to go wrong, I should be in just the same class as Ethelred, no matter how different we should appear to people around us; and the thought frightened me. My mother gave me a great horror of sin, and everything I have heard here has helped to keep me away from it. But sometimes it has seemed impossible for me to do my duty, to do right. Everyday it has grown harder and harder, till sometimes I have become utterly discouraged. Sometimes, too, it has seemed to me that I am conquered, that I have fallen into sin. And all the time there is Ethelred, poor fellow, before me with his want of self-control and with all the ugliness of sin to scare me at the prospect of what I may become."

"And am I to understand, then, Earl, that Ethelred has converted you from the fact that he is a bad boy?"

"That is one of the reasons, Father; but the other reason, and perhaps the principal reason, is that he got me to arguing with him about religion. He spoke so bitterly of Catholics that I lost my temper and began to defend them. Then he attacked different doctrines of the Church, and I couldn't help trying to answer him. It seems he has read a lot of books against Catholic teachings, and he brought up some objections I had never heard before. They stunned me at first."

"And do you want an answer for them yet, my boy?"

"No, Father; I thought out some of the difficulties myself, and I read up the others out of books in our college library. The more we talked, the more I saw how strong was the position of the Catholic Church. In the long run, my reading and thinking and arguing made things so clear to me that I now feel sure that the Catholic Church is the true Church and the only true Church."

"Well, what next, Earl?"

"There's the rub, Father—my promise to my mother."

"Your father was a Catholic, my boy?"

"Yes, sir."

"And your aunt who now has charge of you is a Catholic?"

"Yes, sir."

"And there is no one in authority over you to object to your becoming a Catholic?"

"No, sir."

Father Noland paused for a moment.

"Earl, I know that you believe your mother is in Heaven."

"Father, I think she was a saint of God."

"So do I, my dear boy. Did it ever occur to you, Earl, that she is keeping watch and ward over you? I too, my boy, believe, as I said, that she is in Heaven; and she loves you yet, and prays for you."

"It must be so," said Earl fervently, and oh so gratified. His heart had grown warm within him as much at the manner as at the words of the kind priest.

"Now, Earl, I do not intend to solve your difficulty for you. You can do that for yourself. What you need is more light. If you prepare your heart, God will give it to you. I can help you, I believe, to prepare your heart. Earl, you must go to your teacher and explain your conduct."

"I'd rather not, sir."

"Exactly; it will be a humiliation for you, and God gives light to those who humble themselves. But you must do it; it is your duty. Look at the circumstances for a moment. Since the retreat, you have failed to give satisfaction in class. Your teacher noticed that, but he did not know the troubled and restless state you were in. He was quite right in thinking it his duty to call you to account."

"Perhaps he was, sir."

"Of course he was; you do not wear your heart on your sleeve. According to your own account, you are extremely reticent."

"That's my way, Father."

"Exactly. And again, when Mr. Gade called you to order in class, you took the correction in bad part."

"But he was wrong, sir."

"That is, Earl, he was not infallible. Only God can read the heart. According to all appearances, his action was fully warranted. He acted according to his best judgment, whereas your conduct was dictated by pride."

"Yes; and when he spoke to me so kindly today, Father, I was rude. I'm beginning to be more and more ashamed of myself."

"And your duty is to apologize and explain. There is no doubt in the matter. Think, Earl, of your mother in Heaven, and put the case before her. And I am sure that in your heart you can fancy her answering in but one way. And to your mother, also, you will go about your religious difficulties. As I said, I shall not answer you on that point. The question for you to answer is, what does she wish you to do in the light of her present knowledge—how does she wish you to keep the promise which you made her. You promised to be true to your religion. What is your religion? By the way, Earl, you have, I take it for granted, been baptized?"

"I think so, Father; at least, I've always taken it for granted."

"Most probably you have been. However, on a question so important, one should be contented with nothing less than certainty, so it would be well to look the matter up. Now, Earl, go and pray. And remember, my boy, while you pray, your mother in Heaven is praying with you."

"Thank you very much, Father. I will follow your advice as well as I can. It seems to me that I now begin to see my way. Goodbye, Father."

Earl went to the chapel and threw himself on his knees before a painting of the Good Shepherd. After a little, he deliberately arose and took a position before the statue of the Immaculate Mother. For the first time in his life, Earl found himself raising his troubled heart in love and confidence to her whose sweet intercession never fails of bringing relief.

Chapter XV

*IN WHICH THE DARLING GOES INTO BUSINESS AND
THE MIDGETS INTO BANKRUPTCY*

"WHAT makes you look so cheerful, Earl?" asked Eddie, on the following Sunday afternoon.

"I've had a talk with Mr. Gade, and now everything is all right between us. I wanted to apologize before the whole class, and he wouldn't hear of it. He says if there's any apologizing to be done, he'll do it himself. Then I begged him not to speak about the matter at all, and he has promised. I like him better than ever now. When he explained to me all his reasons for objecting to my conduct, I felt that I had laid myself open to being misunderstood, and that instead of being too hard he had been too easy on me."

"Mr. Gade is a trump," said Eddie, and there was gladness written upon his face.

"It cost me a lot to go up to him, though," continued Earl. I've not done much apologizing in my life, and it doesn't seem to come natural. Last evening, after I had that talk with Father Noland, I went off and prayed and prayed for courage. And I got it from the Blessed Virgin. And now I have to go and pray for one more thing, and I'm going to pray to her again."

"You needn't tell me what it is," said Eddie. "I can guess it. There's only one thing I'd like to suggest."

"What is that?"

Eddie blushed and hummed for a moment.

"Well, you *might* want a Godfather and—and—say, Earl, won't you take me?"

And then the two lads laughed and giggled; but for all their laughing and giggling, one could see that in the hearts of each were a great happiness and a great love.

"Maybe I'll need you, Eddie. I don't see my way yet, but I feel that it may come."

"Surer than Christmas," said Eddie cheerfully.

"Halloa, there's our dear Mama's Darling tackling a small boy!"

They had turned the corner of the classroom building and come suddenly upon two boys. One was Ethelred, the other a very small boy, Willie Reardon by name. Ethelred was holding Willie by the coat and speaking, apparently, with great earnestness. On catching sight of Earl and Eddie, he slunk away with an expression of annoyance on his face, which did not escape the quick eye of Devereux.

"Was the Darling trying to sell you something, Willie?"

"Yes. He had a silver watch chain, which he said was worth over two dollars and fifty cents, and offered it to me for thirty cents."

"Did you buy it?"

"Not for thirty cents. I jewed him down to twenty."

"He tried to sell me that chain," laughed Earl, "for fifty cents. What a fellow he is."

"But wasn't he trying to get something else out of you when we came round the corner?" continued Eddie.

"Yes, he offered to lend me twenty cents cash if I'd pay him twenty-five cents on Tuesday when I get my pocket money. I bought the chain the same way, for twenty cents; but on Tuesday when we get our pocket money, I'm to pay him twenty-five cents."

"Oho!" cried Eddie, his eyes snapping. "Now I'm beginning to understand. Did you notice, Earl, that the Darling has been holding confidential talks with nearly every little chap in the yard?"

"Yes," responded Earl, "now that you speak of it, it does strike me that he has been up to something."

"Up to something!" repeated Eddie. "It's quite clear what he's been up to. Why, the

yard has been flush with money today—
didn't you see the crowd at the candy store,
and the way the pies went? And think of its
being a Sunday—five days since the fellows
got their pocket money."

"That is strange," said Earl, "especially
since I collected fifteen cents from every boy
last Tuesday for the football fund."

"And that is precisely what has helped on
Ethelred's plans. He saw that the small boys
were hungry and hard up this morning, and
he's been lending them twenty cents or so,
provided they pay him back twenty-five cents
next Tuesday."

"It's a regular confidence game!" cried Earl,
indignantly. "I'll stop that thing right now,
even if I have to pay the extra money myself.
If there's anything I hate, it is imposing on
a little boy. Why, that fellow is as selfish
as—confound it, I'll go and see him at once
and give him a piece of my mind!"

"No you don't, Earl," said Eddie, catching
his indignant friend by the arm. "Just wait
till we've talked it over. I think I see a way
of fixing the matter without any trouble.
There's no use in fighting when fun will
answer just as well. Now look here, Willie
Reardon, you see the way things are, don't
you?"

"I see that the Darling has been working us little boys for all we're worth," answered Willie ruefully. "I know two fellows he lent fifteen cents to, and he is to get a quarter back from each."

"Well," whispered Eddie, poking his index finger into Willie's face, "I want you to keep quiet for a while. If you talk, you'll spoil the fun, and besides, you'll lose money. Just leave the matter to me and Earl and Roger, and you'll find that everything will turn out all right. Now, you'll keep quiet, won't you?"

"Of course."

"Very well; clear off now, and tell Roger Haines we want to see him right away. Earl, I've got a grand scheme. Listen."

Ed fell into a whisper and unfolded his plan. Earl, as he listened, actually laughed. Presently, Roger came up and was admitted into their confidence. For nearly an hour did the three conspirators put their heads together; and when they had come to an agreement, they were as jolly a trio of boys as could be found.

In a body they went up to the treasurer's room. They entered giggling, and even after the door had closed them in, anyone passing along the corridor could hear now and then a merry laugh. And the loudest laugher of them all was the treasurer himself. Father Harter, the treasurer of Henryton College, was a hale old man with a clear eye and a venerable face. He had been dealing his life long with boys; and having been, so rumor ran, a harum-scarum himself, he could sympathize with wild boys; and being a man of tender heart and generous sentiment, he loved and was loved by every student with whom he came into contact. Only one charge had ever been lodged against the grayheaded, cheerful old Father: he was too lenient in his judgment. If God could err, it would be on the side of leniency.

The three boys came out presently, and it was evident from their faces that Father Harter had entered heartily into their scheme.

Although they talked together confidentially at all odd moments on the following day, Devereux, nevertheless, contrived to keep close watch on Ethelred. This young gentleman was behaving strangely. There was an air of restlessness about him. He held two secret conferences with Farwell, the day scholar, and during the second received from him a letter. Eddie saw the envelope slipped stealthily from Farwell's hand to the other's, and he felt almost sure that something was wrong. Had he but seen the address upon the envelope, his suspicions would have received the strongest confirmation.

"I'm willing to bet the money that I lent the Darling against five cents that Ethelred is going to run away again," he said to his two chums.

"Oh, he'll not do that," said Earl. "There would be no sense in his running away after that first attempt of his. It doesn't stand to reason. Why did he come back? And now why should he want to run off again? There's no sense in the matter."

"If you go to reasoning about it, you have me," answered Ed. "But all the same, he's going to go—and soon, too. He has been getting things together, and borrowing right and left, and he's been studying up the best way to get out of here. He tackled several fellows about it."

"That reminds me," said Earl. "He took a walk with me on the road back of the college a little before dinner this morning, and he seemed very much interested in the trees that line it. He remarked that it would be easy for a boy to slip out through the back gate and take the road for a hundred yards or so and then turn and cut across a few fields to the village. Then I asked him whether he was thinking of running away again, and he began to protest most eagerly that he had not the least thought of doing so, till I shut him up. It didn't occur to me then that there was anything back of his eagerness; but now that you have spoken, Ed, I begin to think that he wasn't quite natural."

"Exactly," assented Ed. "He protests too much."

"It's pretty clear," put in Roger, "that if the Darling intends running away again, he's not going to publish it on the housetops."

"If there's anyone knows it," added Earl, "it is Farwell. He's a crooked day scholar, and whenever a tough character gets into our yard, Farwell always becomes his chief friend."

"I think he won't run away till tomorrow night," continued Ed. "He won't go today because if he did, he would go off minus all the money he lent. Tomorrow he collects everything that is due him. As far as I can make out, he counts on making nearly two dollars on his various loans and bargains."

"He has a lot of clothes belonging to me," added Earl.

"And he borrowed a pen knife and a necktie of me," said Roger.

"And he wanted to borrow my rubber coat," said Devereux, "and he got the rubber. Excuse the slang, but we must have our little joke. Well," he continued, "everything is fixed for tomorrow morning, I believe. And during the day, we can study up Ethelred's plans for getting away from here. I'm afraid," he added, as the bell rang for night studies, "that I'll study more Ethelred than lessons tonight. If he were to stay here much longer, I should lose my class standing. Good night, boys. Just try to keep alive till tomorrow morning."

And indeed they were very much alive the next day when, after breakfast, they scampered from the refectory to the corridor on which was situated the treasurer's office. Every boy in the small yard took part in that scampering, each one endeavoring to get a position nearest the treasurer's room. Within two minutes after leaving the refectory, the junior students were all drawn up in line, pushing and tugging and pinching and sparring, after the manner of their kind.

The first lad in the line, Eddie Devereux, had knocked softly: once, twice, thrice. But there came no answer. He was about to knock again when the third boy in the line anticipated him by reaching forward and giving the door a violent blow with his clinched fist. He then slipped back into his place, leaving Eddie to take the consequences.

The pushing and tugging ceased like magic, and all awaited in expectant silence the result.

Father Harter threw open his door with some energy and glared severely down the line. Ethelred, who stood at the very end, keeping watch upon the door which led to the yard, was perceptibly nervous. He quailed before the look upon the treasurer's face.

"What do you mean by knocking that way on my door, Eddie Devereux?" cried Father Harter, with much fierceness of manner.

"It was a mistake," said Ed.

"And what do all you boys want at this time of the day?"

"It's Tuesday morning, Father!" exclaimed Peter Lane, who was far down the line.

"Well, suppose it is; what about it?"

"Pocket money day!" cried at least twenty voices.

"Not today!" said Father Harter. "Owing to certain circumstances, none of you extravagant boys gets one cent of pocket money this morning."

And Father Harter stepped back into his room, closed the door and turned the key in the lock.

Some groaned, some laughed; a few, who were in the joke, along with Earl, Eddie and Roger, looked rueful. As for Ethelred, he broke out into a volley of muttered curses. His face had grown pale and his fingers were clutching at the lapels of his coat. He was in a state of intense excitement.

"Hey there! You fellows don't get out this door," he bawled at Peter Lane and five or six other small boys, "until you've paid me my money!"

"Who owes you money?" asked Devereux.

"These fellows," said Ethelred, pointing out the eleven midgets of the yard.

While he was pointing out his debtors, Roger slipped over to Ed and whispered in his ear.

"Do you notice it's the third eleven of the football association to a man?"

"Yes; and I catch the idea, too. Darling," he added aloud, "I'd advise you to clear the way. These little fellows won't stand much nonsense; you'd better let them out."

"Not till we've settled this affair," snarled Ethelred. "I'll spank any one of them if they try to go till I'm done."

"Give him the wedge," whispered Ed to Peter, the captain of the eleven.

Peter's eyes sparkled—a whisper ran

through the bunch of midgets, and at once there were eleven pairs of eyes sparkling as one.

"Line up!" yelled Peter, falling back nine or ten yards from the spot where Ethelred stood with clenched fists.

Ethelred's eyes opened very wide, and his jaw dropped in wonder, when the midgets fell into their places for a rush.

"Seven—eight—eleven—thirteen—twenty-two—keep your feathers on!" bawled Peter in his highest pipe.

A wedge-shaped body of boys shot toward Ethelred, while Peter, detaching himself from the mass, came tripping quietly about the right end. Ethelred did not notice Peter; his eyes were fixed on the wedge. With a bellow, and putting his head down like a bull, he went three paces forward toward the approaching mass. While his foot was still raised for the fourth pace, Peter threw himself straight at his knees, plunging forward as a diver plunges into the water. Peter was a fearless tackler, and fearlessness is the secret of good tackling. In an instant, the two were rolling upon the ground—Peter to the left, the Darling to the right—while between them, with a ringing hurrah, moved the wedge out through the door and into the yard; while the boys within, looking on, forgetting the rules of the corridor, broke into the liveliest expressions of applause.

Peter and Ethelred struggled with all haste to their feet; but Peter was the quicker artist, and darted off for the door, followed at a distance of several yards by the furious Darling.

"Are you hurt?" cried Devereux, catching one of Ethelred's arms.

"Just let me dust you," said Roger, catching the other.

"We'll *all* dust you," put in a third; and Ethelred found himself hemmed in by eighteen or nineteen youths, their faces full of sympathy, and such of their hands as could come into play beating upon his clothes.

A door opened at the further end of the corridor. Father Howard's face appeared, and the next moment every boy had somehow or other got back into the yard.

"It's too bad, Darling," said Devereux, linking his arm with Ethelred's, while the other students, in obedience to a wink from him, left the two to themselves.

"I'm swindled," croaked Ethelred.

"Did they promise to pay you today?"

"Yes, and I insist on their paying!"

"How much do they owe you?"

"Four dollars and fifty cents."

"Do you know how much each one owes you?"

"You just bet I do. Here." Ethelred, as he spoke, pulled a paper from his pocket. "This is a list of the boys who owe me, and the amount they owe."

"And you insist on their paying today?"

"Yes, I do. I've got to have that money before ni—that is, I must have that money; I want to buy a pair of shoes."

"Very well; I'll see whether I can't arrange matters. I'll take this list along and will do the best I can for you."

"Midgets ahoy!" called Ed, leaving the Darling disconsolate upon a bench. The midgets to a man came flocking about Devereux. They scented fun from afar.

"There will be a meeting of the people who are in debt to Ethelred Preston right now in the playroom. All other boys will keep out."

At a run the midgets made for the playroom.

"The meeting is called to order," said Ed presently, with much gravity. "Johnnie Martin, take that chewing gum out of your mouth. Albert Winslow, please to sit straight. Keep quiet there, Jimmie Keller. Now listen while I read this paper."

The following boys have promised to pay me the following amounts on Tuesday morning:

Peter Lane	50 cts.	lent to him	40
William Reardon	50 cts.	" " "	40
Albert Winslow	25 cts.	" " "	15
Vincent Meade	75 cts.	" " "	55
Johnnie Martin	25 cts.	" " "	15
Jimmie Keller	25 cts.	" " "	15
Joe Keller	50 cts.	" " "	40
David Arthur	50 cts.	" " "	35
John Short	25 cts.	" " "	20
Eddie Hastings	25 cts.	" " "	15
Bernard Cassidy	<u>50 cts.</u>	" " "	<u>40</u>
Total	$4.50		$3.30
	<u>3.30</u>		
Net gain	$1.20		

Ethelred Preston

P. S. Vincent Meade is a soft one. He has lots of money, and it's easy to get it from him. The whole lot of them is precious green, and I intend to make a nuther doller or to out of them. E. P.

This postscript, Eddie, for prudential reasons, did not read to the midgets.

"Now, is that all right?" inquired Eddie, raising his eyes from the paper.

Each of the midgets answered affirmatively.

"And according to the agreement you are all bound to pay today?"

"That's so," said Peter.

"Well, there's only one course left for you."

The midgets were now serious.

"You must go into bankruptcy—you must make an assignment. You must appoint a receiver."

What big eyes the midgets had! They sat silent and solemn.

"I'll be your receiver, if you've no objections," continued Ed suavely.

"All right," said several. "How are you going to do it?"

"Let me explain," said Eddie. When people owe money and are called upon to pay, and can't do it, they are forced into bankruptcy. That's just your fix. You owe money and can't pay. You are obliged to pay what you can, and if Ethelred has no objection, you can go into business again. I must arrange that with him myself. Now, go through your pockets carefully and gather up all your money and pass it over to me."

Peter found a penny in the lining of his coat, put it in his hat and, then going around, gathered in the small change from those who had any.

"Forty cents in all," said Devereux. "Boys, as far as I can make out, each of you will pay eight cents on the dollar; that is, those who owe the Darling fifty cents will satisfy by paying four cents, and those who owe twenty-five cents by paying two cents."

He took out his notebook and made a calculation.

"At that rate I find that your debts will be paid off for thirty-six cents."

"And what'll you do with the other four cents?" asked Johnnie Martin, a serious boy with a sharp face.

"I shall keep that for my commission," said Ed, cheerfully.

"Do you mean to say," continued Martin, "that after you pay the Darling those thirty-six cents, we don't owe him anything more?"

"Not exactly; only don't let on to him or the joke will be spoiled. A bankrupt should pay his debts as soon as he can. You people should pay Ethelred what remains due to him as soon as you get your pocket-money."

The midgets all looked relieved—they were honest youngsters. They were delighted, too, for they now saw that a good joke was on foot.

"I shall now, if you have no objections, young gentlemen, go over and try to fix up accounts with the Darling," continued Eddie.

He arose and, followed by the crowd, crossed the yard.

"Ethelred Preston, you insist on payment?"

"Yes, I do."

"Well, those little fellows can't pay their debts in full, and as you insist on full payment, they have been forced to make an assignment and have gone into bankruptcy."

Ethelred stared stolidly.

"Well, I don't care whether they go into bankruptcy or not. I want my money—that's all."

"And as they have gone into bankruptcy," pursued Devereux, "they have appointed me their receiver."

"Are you going to pay me my money?" inquired Ethelred, with no little eagerness.

"Ethelred Preston, as receiver for the young gentlemen commonly called the midgets, I find that their assets amount to forty cents and their liabilities to four dollars and a half. You shall be paid eight cents on the dollar. Here it is—thirty-six cents."

"I won't take it," said Ethelred, angrily. "Think I'm a fool?"

"I'll not tell you what I think. You should not ask questions like that. But you've got to take it; it's the law."

"Get out!" squawked Ethelred.

"You will notice that we *are* out. Here's the money."

"I'll not take one cent!" howled Ethelred, and to the astonishment of many, his face began to twitch as though he were about to cry. After all, Ethelred had his feelings too.

This unexpected exhibition confused Eddie. He was a tender-hearted boy and could face anything but tears. He paused to think. The joke was too hard on Ethelred. Devereux had intended going much further, but he could not do a cruel thing.

"Oh, well, Preston," he said, "you'll get all your money, if you only wait."

"But I can't wait. I want it now."

"Well, then, come along with me to Father Harter. He'll fix it for you."

And Ed, followed by Preston, proceeded to the treasurer's room.

Ethelred did not get his claim allowed in full. There was no net gain of one dollar and twenty cents. He received what he had lent and went out with mixed feelings. His speculation had failed, but at any rate he had come by his own.

Then the midgets were summoned to Father Harter's presence.

"See here, you boys," he began with a severity so pronounced that every lad in the room saw its insincerity, "you deserve a good trouncing, every one of you."

"That's so, Father," said Peter Lane sweetly, catching one end of Father Harter's cincture, while Johnnie Martin fondled the other end.

Father Harter's face twitched. It was hard work for him to be stern with the ingenuous American small boy.

"You needn't think I'm going to give you any pocket money now. I have just paid off your debts, and you may get along the best way you can for one week."

"O Father!" There were eleven voices in this cry of deprecation.

"I mean what I say. You boys have got to learn sense. There now, you can go."

Then spoke up Vincent Meade, the fullback of the midgets.

"See here, Father Harter; you can't fool us. We know you're not angry."

"Yes I am, sir." Again there was a slight twitching at the lips.

The boys began to smile sweetly.

"No, you're not. You couldn't get mad at Peter Lane and Johnnie Martin if you tried."

"Get out of here, every one of you! Do you hear me? Get out at once!" This time there was a twinkle in Father Harter's eye, and the midgets knew that he was lost.

"We'll not go out till you laugh, Father," said Vincent.

Another twitch, another twinkle, and it was all over with the jolly treasurer of Henryton College. He laughed long to a very effective treble accompaniment. By the way, what a deal of laughing choruses we have been obliged to chronicle since the opening of this modest story.

"How much are you going to give us, Father? Let's have our twenty-five cents just the same as though nothing had happened," pursued Meade.

There was a great deal of arguing before this question had been settled. Finally, the midgets departed smiling and radiant, each one short just five cents of his regular weekly allowance.

Some of my readers may consider Father Harter as a weak man in dealing with the students. In this they will agree with Peter Lane.

"We can do what we like with him!" said Peter triumphantly, as the procession scurried into the yard.

And yet there was not a boy in the crowd who was not the better and happier for this good Father's so-called weakness. For his weakness was the weakness which is strength. In matters of conduct and of duty, Father Harter could bend these boys as he pleased. At his suggestion, the stubborn boy became docile, the discouraged boy took heart of grace, the proud spirit humbled itself and prayerless lips were molded to earnest calls upon God. What others did with punishment and long labor, he did without effort. What others utterly failed in, he accomplished with laborless triumph. And yet the secret of his success is not far to seek. He loved boys and sympathized with them.

Chapter XVI

*IN WHICH EDDIE DEVEREUX BECOMES
A GODFATHER*

ON Tuesday afternoon, Earl knocked at Father Noland's door.

"What makes you look so happy, my boy?" asked Father Noland, with the genial smile which was ever ready on the appearance of his boy friends.

"Because, Father," answered Earl, taking a chair which the Father motioned him to, "my difficulty is gone; and I am now ready to be a Catholic."

"You feel quite sure of your position?"

"Yes, Father; and it came about in a way that looks providential. Yesterday and the day before, I went to the chapel and prayed hard for light. I thought of my mother, and it seemed to me that she too wanted me to be a Catholic. After praying, I felt almost certain that it was my duty to do so. But I thought it would not hurt to wait until today for more light. Father, it has come in the queerest way imaginable."

"How so, Earl?"

"At noon today, I got a letter from my old nurse in reply to mine. It seems that she was commissioned while I was a little baby to see to my being baptized by a Lutheran clergyman. It was several weeks after my birth, and as my mother was still sick in bed, it was thought advisable not to put off my Baptism till her recovery. The nurse started off to bring me to the church. My father met her on the way and bribed her to bring me back and pretend that I had been baptized. I suppose he intended to have me baptized by a Catholic priest later on, but for some reason or other it appears that he neglected doing so. So, Father, I am not even a Lutheran. Just think of it! I can now start out with a clean record. I have tried to be a good boy, but I have missed it sometimes; and now once I am baptized, the ugliness of the past is over forever. If I could have it my way, I'd be baptized at once and die."

"What a strange story!" said Father Noland.

"Isn't it? You remember when I came to see you last, how you advised me to look up the question of my Baptism? I wrote at once to my old nurse. She answered on the instant of receiving it. She writes that the thing has been on her conscience ever since. My father, she says, being a Catholic, wanted me to be baptized by a priest and promised her that he would see to it. He intended to at the time, but he kept on putting it off and off till finally nothing was done. You can imagine how the letter surprised me. On reading it, every doubt was gone at once. My mother had asked me to promise to be true to my religion. She knows now, and I do, that my religion is *the* religion."

"You have answered the difficulty, Earl. Your mother's wish was that you should be true to the *true* religion, and were she to appear to you now, she would bless your choice."

"Father, I should like to be baptized tomorrow. It would be better *today*, if I were prepared, but I want some time to get ready. I am happy now, but I know that tomorrow will be the happiest day of my life."

Father Noland took the boy's hand in his. He too was happy beyond expression.

"I want Eddie Devereux for my Godfather," continued Earl.

"Of course. And what about your First Communion?"

"Couldn't I make it right after Baptism? I am ready, Father. You know I have been here three years and have paid attention to the Catechism instructions, especially this year."

Father Noland considered this point for several minutes.

"Earl, next Friday will be the first Friday of the month, the day of the Sacred Heart. Suppose you put off your Communion till then. Tomorrow I will baptize you after Mass, and then during that and the next day, you may get ready for Communion. Not that you do not know enough to receive the Blessed Eucharist, but in order that you may prepare your heart the better."

"And that will be another red-letter day in my life," said Earl. "Yes, I like the plan.

I've always had a love for the Sacred Heart devotion, and besides, I can prepare for my General Confession."

"You make no General Confession, my boy."

"How is that, Father?"

"Because Confession is for the sins committed *after* Baptism. You may go to Confession next Thursday night, if you wish, to tell all about what has happened since Wednesday morning; but as regards anything that occurred before your Baptism, that will never be matter for absolution."

Earl looked still happier.

"That makes it so easy for me," he said. "Of course, I was willing to tell all the sins of my life, but it seemed such a hard job; and then I was afraid I might leave out something important. But now it is so nice and easy. Father, I must go off and tell Eddie."

Eddie was far more effusive in his expressions of joy than Father Noland. As it happened, he had received three dollars from home at noon, and he at once treated every boy he could find. Very quickly the news of Earl's conversion went around, and many warm and loving hearts rejoiced that the hero of the yard was about to receive the lovely baptismal robe.

"I say, Earl," said Eddie, later on in the

afternoon, "we're going to have some great fun tonight, but I suppose we had better count you out of it. It's about Ethelred, you know."

"Have you learned anything more?"

"Yes, a great deal. One of the little boys heard the Darling telling that little wretch Farwell that all was fixed and that he saw his way clear to getting away. Other fellows saw Ethelred steal out into Mapletree road back of the College. He had several packages when he went out, and he disappeared in a clump of trees some distance down. When he came back again the bundles were gone. His box in the washroom is empty, and he has been arranging his desk in the study hall."

"So he goes tonight, then?"

"Yes, there's scarcely a doubt about the matter. He'll not leave before recess after second hour, otherwise he might be missed and sent for before the train passes."

"And do you intend to let him run away?"

"Yes," said Eddie; "he'll go sure this time, and I'll bet anything he'll not come back. But all the same, I think we'll manage to have some fun."

"How, Eddie?"

"I don't want to distract you, Earl. You go

ahead and get ready for your Baptism, and tomorrow morning, if things go the way I expect, I shall have a great story to tell you."

Chapter XVII

*IN WHICH THE DARLING RUNS AWAY
IN GOOD EARNEST*

"RECESS!" announced the study-keeper. At the word, the silence, which had been sensitive to the scratching of a pen, was broken by the shutting of books, the slamming of desks, the shifting of chairs and of feet; and in a moment the noise, with its makers, was transferred to the yard. The study-keeper cast a glance down the aisles and, satisfied that all the students had left the room, took his departure.

His footfalls were still sounding upon the pavement outside when a head bobbed up from behind a bench and two small eyes glanced warily about. Satisfied that the coast was clear, the owner of the small eyes, no other than Ethelred Preston, awoke to sudden activity. Going to certain desks, he helped himself hurriedly to three or four fountain pens, a box of letter-paper, a gold pen, a silver watch, and a few odds and ends. He then thoughtfully put on a fine, heavy overcoat—the best in the hall—which happened to be Earl Meriwether's. He took the coat without malice. He had no particular grudge against Earl; but Earl's coat was the best, and he chose it as a matter of business.

Satisfied that under the limitations of time and place he had done his best, Ethelred threw open one of the windows on the side opposite the playground and leaped out. Pausing for a short time to assure himself that there was no one near, he made his way under the long shadows of the trees to the back gate of the college. As he went along, he could hear the shouts of the boys in the yard. From the shadows he could see them running about in the moonlight. The prefects were both in full view of his eyes, but at satisfactory distances.

Crouching at the gate, the amiable Ethelred shook both fists at the yard and the inmates thereof, and then slipped out of the college grounds.

"Now I'm safe," he grunted, as he reached the first of the line of maples and, retiring into its shadow, mopped the perspiration from his brow. It was a chilly night, but Ethelred was not sensible to the cold as yet.

Having regained his breath, he started down the road, keeping to the side where the shadows lay thickest. The moon shone clear and full, throwing a ghastly white light upon the middle of the way. There was no wind; not a branch stirred; and the silence about him was accentuated by the shouts of the lads in the playground. Ethelred could hear his own breathing, and it frightened him. He stopped once more to regain his breath.

As he stood still, there suddenly came, or seemed to come, upon his ears a low groan. Was it imagination? He could hear his heart-beats now, and down his back there swept an odd, chilly sensation. He listened again, but all was silent.

"I'm scared," he said. He spoke aloud to reassure himself by the sound of his own voice. "I won't stop anymore." And walking swiftly, he made toward a clump of trees some rods further down.

As he advanced, he heard, or fancied he heard, a movement as of stealthy footsteps on the further side of the trees which lined the way. But he gave no heed to these real or fancied sounds. He felt sure that it was his disturbed imagination. No one ever frequented this road except the students of the College, and they were now on their way to their night prayers.

At length, the clump of trees and the underbrush were reached. Pushing through the weeds, Ethelred made for an old stump standing out plainly in the light; and scattering aside with his hands some dried twigs and leaves, he uncovered to the moon a large valise.

As the burnished bands glittered in the light, Ethelred gave a sob of relief.

"*Now* I'm all right."

He raised the valise in his hands; it was heavy.

"*Your money or your life!*"

At the words uttered in a low, guttural, disguised voice, the valise dropped from Ethelred's hands, his blood seemed to freeze in his veins, and there was a horrible, stinging sensation about the roots of his hair. His eyes lifted once, and then he fell back flat upon the ground.

Five weird figures had hemmed him in— five unearthly figures. To Ethelred's eyes they seemed to be giants. Black masks were on their faces; high conical hats covered their heads. Long robes reached from their shoulders to their feet. They stood like statues, each with one hand upon the hip, and the other holding a pistol pointed at the unhappy youth. No wonder he fell.

"Get up, and as you value your life, don't open your mouth!" came the same unnatural voice.

Ethelred arose, and staggered as he stood.

"Put up your hands!"

The boy obeyed; and while four of the strange figures continued to bear themselves like statues, the one who had spoken came forward, carried away the valise, and then examined Ethelred's pockets.

He went about it slowly, while not a figure moved. Ethelred's hands continued high in the air; he breathed heavily and wished in his heart that one of those figures would move or cough—anything rather than the silence and the pointed pistols.

It was a long search, for Ethelred's pockets were many and all of them were well-stored. The collection made a little heap—pencils, knives, money, ties, cuff buttons, three watches and all manner of little knickknacks.

Next the examiner took off Ethelred's overcoat, then his vest. Stepping aside, he returned with other clothes upon his arm. These he handed to Ethelred, motioning him to put them on.

With trembling fingers, and breathing heavily, Ethelred made an endeavor to put on the vest.

Oh, if he could but open his mouth! He was suffocating—he could not even swallow. But to open his mouth, as he understood the leader's words, meant death. The vest slipped from his clasp, while fresh drops of perspiration broke out upon his face. The silent robber then took the overcoat and threw it over Ethelred's shoulders, and placing the vest and coat upon one of the nerveless arms, he slipped two silver dollars into his hands, which, however nervous their owner might be, instinctively closed upon them tight.

"Count twenty; then run for your life, and don't dare open your mouth till you have reached the station! But first, turn your face toward the village and don't look back!" came the sepulchral tones of the leader.

While the figures, thus far motionless, lowered their pistols and massed themselves between Ethelred and the College, Ethelred tried to count twenty conscientiously. He must have broken down and begun again five or six times; he certainly counted twenty.

When he felt quite sure that he had followed this injunction, he took to his heels;

and as he started, there came behind him a loud, deafening explosion which lent him winged speed. In the time that it takes to narrate it, Ethelred had disappeared from the view of his ghostly persecutors.

"Well!" exclaimed the leader, throwing off his mask and revealing the merry face of Ed Devereux, "wasn't it a grand success?"

"Stunning!" said Roger Haines, removing his weird, conical cap.

"If he runs that way," added a third, "he'll catch the train without any trouble at all."

"Oh, but boys!" cried Eddie, with eyes that sparkled above their wonted sparkle, "we've done a great night's work! I knew that Ethelred was going to run away in Earl Meriwether's clothes and with a few knickknacks borrowed here and there, but I didn't think he was going to rob right and left. I could hardly keep from saying something when I took my own fountain pen and my own gold sleeve buttons out of his pocket."

"And I felt like putting in an oar," broke in the fourth highwayman, "when you brought out my box of writing paper. It was a birthday gift from my aunt, and each sheet of paper had my initials stamped on it."

The boys meanwhile had been doffing their weird attire and now stood revealed, five young gentlemen in the last stages of the knickerbocker period of life. They were radiantly happy. The fact that Ethelred had been scared out of his wits dashed not their merriment in the least. He was a thief, a sneak-thief, they agreed, and the frightening which he had received was a very light punishment.

And then the romance of the thing! Moonlight! Playing at highwaymen! Pistols! They were toy pistols, which do very well at night! It was a real adventure, something that could be talked about and laughed over till examination time, and recalled and laughed over in maturer years as one of the most interesting experiences of their college life.

"Wasn't that 'giant firecracker' a success, though!" cried Ed. "It sounded like a cannon. The Darling gave a leap into the air when it went off, and then he just flew. Oh, but this is a picnic!"

"Talk about circuses!" chimed in Roger ecstatically.

"But wasn't it good of Father Howard to let us out!" continued Ed. "I told him that there was some thieving going on and that I felt sure I could stop it if he'd let me take you four and stay out from second hour's studies and night prayers. I gave him my word of honor that we would behave all right and not go beyond this roadway and said that we'd be back before the boys were asleep. So, boys, gather up the spoils, and we'll go in and report."

Father Howard was not a little surprised when the dauntless five filed into his room and placed upon his desk one large tightly packed valise and any number of odds and ends.

"What's all this?" he asked.

"Stolen goods, mostly, Father, I think," Eddie replied. "Of course, some of the things may be Ethelred's, but we didn't have time to find out."

"Ethelred's!" repeated Father Howard.

"Yes—his mama's darling!"

"And where is Ethelred?"

"I *think* he's on the train by this time, in an old overcoat, and with just about money enough to bring him home. We didn't mind taking everything of value he had because we felt pretty sure that most of it was stolen, and we knew that whatever was his could be returned along with his trunk."

"Well, suppose you tell me all about it."

Devereux told his story with a zest, and Father Howard listened with unaffected interest and delight.

"When I hear a thing like that," said the

vice president at the end of the recital, "I can hardly keep from wishing I was a boy again. Now you may all go to the infirmary, and tomorrow morning take a late sleep. You have had a great deal of fun and done a good deed, too. Tomorrow I shall try to find out who owns all these things and send what is unclaimed to Ethelred. Good night, boys; I am very much obliged to you indeed."

"So," soliloquized the Father, gazing at the valise, which bore the initials of Peter Lane, "this is the end of Ethelred Preston."

The prefect of the college had made the like remark on a like occasion. He was mistaken. As the sequel will show, Father Howard was mistaken too.

Chapter XVIII

A MEMORABLE MORNING

ON the following day, while the students of Henryton College were at their breakfast, Earl Meriwether was solemnly baptized into the Catholic Church. At his request, no one was present, with the exception of Eddie, the happiest of Godfathers, Roger Haines, and four others of his classmates. Earl's face, as the services proceeded, was aglow with holy joy; and when Father Noland poured the regenerating water upon his head and pronounced in solemn and fervent tones the sacramental words, Earl, realizing the beauty of the invisible garment put upon his soul and the sweet union between himself and the most Blessed Trinity, could not restrain his tears. It was the second time since his entering college that Devereux had seen Earl weep. Five days ago his tears had been tears of anguish; now they were tears of supreme joy.

*　　*　　*　　*　　*

There was a special breakfast prepared for Earl and his five companions. On the center of the table, a beautiful lily bowed its perfect chalice, and three splendid roses blushed before the blushing neophyte. Around Earl's plate were grouped a prayerbook, a pair of beads, a Sacred Heart badge, a silver medal of the Immaculate Conception [Miraculous Medal] and an ivory crucifix.

"They're all yours, Godson," said Eddie, who wanted to dance. "The prayerbook is from the

Godfather, the beads from Father Noland, the crucifix from Roger and the medal from Peter Lane. The flowers are from the other fellows here, and just sit down and pitch in." He added enthusiastically, "There are biscuits for breakfast, and all the butter a fellow can use!"

It was a merry breakfast. They talked of many things, but finally settled upon the departed Darling and, once upon that topic, never left it.

"Just think," said Eddie, "he came here last Thursday morning—not quite a week yet, and it seems as though he had been here three weeks."

"He woke us up," said Roger.

"That's so," assented Ed. "Things were getting awfully dull when he came along. We hadn't had any fun to speak of since the Christmas holidays."

"I've noticed," said Earl, "that the month of January is generally the dullest month of the school year."

"But this month wasn't," said Ed. "It would have been, only for the Darling. When he came along I was so dead that I was thinking of applying for a burial permit. But since that time, everything has been on the go."

"Very much so," added Roger. "First, on the day he came, Earl got into that row with Mr. Gade."

"Oh, that reminds me," broke in Ed. "Mr. Gade gave me something for you, and I came near forgetting all about it." Eddie pulled out an envelope, as he spoke, and handed it to Earl.

Earl opened it and found that it contained a picture and some verses.

"Did Mr. Gade write a poem for you, Earl?" asked Father Noland.

Earl, before replying, ran his eyes over the manuscript.

"Yes, Father," he made answer, "and it seems to be very beautiful. Isn't it kind of him?"

"More kind of him than you think, Earl; for Mr. Gade, though a poet, is very chary of his verses. I wanted him to write something for me lately, and he answered by quoting a few lines from a young Englishman named William Watson who, with Thompson, promises to take the highest place among the poets of the day. Mr. Gade had Watson's book fresh from the publisher upon his desk, and said as he closed it:

> Not mine the rich and showering hand,
>   that strews
> The facile largess of a stintless muse.
> A fitful presence, seldom tarrying long,
> Capriciously she touches me to song—

> Then leaves me to lament her flight in
>   vain,
> And wonder will she ever come again.

"And then, Earl, he added, 'If I have an hour to spare, I shall give it to my dear pupil, Earl Meriwether.' You may rest assured, then, that aside from the occasion, Mr. Gade's verses are well worthy of being treasured. Probably, the older you grow, the more you will appreciate them."

"I believe you, sir." And Earl put the envelope with its enclosure very carefully away.

"Well," resumed Roger, "just think of all that has happened since Ethelred arrived. After Ethelred's trouble in the morning, we had a boxing match at noon. Then Ethelred passes a new examination under the direction of Peter Sullivan and Ed Land. Next he goes to bed in the music teacher's room and is quiet for half a day. Then he climbs down a rope."

"And don't forget to remember," put in Ed Devereux, "that he stole twenty feet of it and I had to pay the damages. Go on, Roger; only please try not to tire out my Godson."

"And then when we think we're done with him, he bobs up serenely in the dormitory next morning and at studies is introduced to us as a reformed runaway."

"And after that," added Devereux, "he kept us on the jump for three days to find out what he was up to. But there's one thing I feel sorry for. It's the first time since I've been here that I was ever thrown in with a student who was a thief. It's so disgusting to live near such a fellow. Last night when I was searching him and pulling out things that belonged to the boys I knew, I felt very much like setting the whole crowd on him to give him a pounding; I'm very glad I didn't yield. It would have been an act of revenge and the conduct of a savage."

"Ethelred has been formally expelled, I hear," said Roger.

"I feel bad for his poor mother," said Earl. "The boy will break her heart. She is a very refined woman, and I can't understand how Ethelred could live under her care and be what he is."

"By the way, Earl," said Eddie, helping himself to another biscuit, "the Darling went off in your overcoat, coat and vest."

"Did he have my overcoat too? I lent him the other things and am not surprised at his taking them, but I am surprised that he should take my coat."

"He's the first boy I ever came across who had no sense of gratitude at all," said Roger

Haines, putting down his knife and fork. "Why, just think of the way he's acted with Earl Meriwether! Earl has been doing everything to make him feel at home. He lent him clothes, gave him postage stamps, treated him to candy a dozen times, and he went with him when the other boys fought shy of him. The last thing in return for all this is that the Darling makes off with his overcoat. It's downright disgusting. I didn't think there were any boys made that way."

"A great deal of the selfishness and ingratitude in the world," said Father Noland, "is to be accounted for by a passion for money-getting. People who allow the love of money to grow upon them soon come to lose their love for everything else. Few boys have such a passion for gain as Ethelred seems to have."

"Well, he's done anyhow," Eddie observed.

"And he'll not show his face here again," added Haines. "There's not a single boy in the yard would touch him with a ten-foot pole."

"Poor fellow!" said Earl. "We are abusing him when we ought to pity him. He was an unhappy boy when he was here, and he was unhappy when he left. I feel sorry for him."

And with this charitable comment, Earl rose and, forgetting Ethelred on the moment, put himself to preparing for the First Friday.

Chapter XIX

ETHELRED PRESTON, BRIGHTON, ALBANY VILLA

IT was the noon recess on Thursday morning. The small boys, with the exception of a few stragglers, were all gathered together discussing the disappearance of Ethelred Preston and examining the various articles, just restored to them, which the Darling had attempted to run away with.

"Halloa!" said Peter Lane, suddenly. "Here comes Earl Meriwether, and there's something queer about his face."

"He looks puzzled, and he's going to tell us some news," said Johnny Martin, the sharp-eyed.

"What is it, Earl?" cried Peter.

"Boys, I have the most extraordinary news."

Every head was fixed in attention.

"Ethelred Preston is back again."

The boys stood as though they had been cast into a trance.

"He's in the parlor with Father Edmunds," Earl went on.

The listeners began to look at each other with puzzled faces.

"Is he to be arrested, Earl?" inquired Devereux.

"It seems not. I haven't seen Ethelred yet.

But I just now met Father Howard, and he was laughing. I don't see yet why he was laughing. He contrived to tell me, between his laughs, that fifteen minutes ago, the man at the door brought the president of the college a card that read:

> Master Ethelred Preston,
> Albany Villa, Brighton
> [At Home Tuesdays]

"And what did Father Edmunds do when he got that card?" inquired Haines.

"When Father Edmunds got the card, he ordered his secretary to telephone for a policeman."

There was a sigh of relief from the auditors.

"Then Father Edmunds waited till the policeman came and asked him to stay in the hall outside the parlor for a moment. The president entered the parlor and came out in a minute and told the policeman that there would be no need of his services."

"O-O-O-Oh!" This was but one of the many expressions of astonishment which this announcement provoked.

"But I haven't told you the strangest part yet. Father Howard says that not only has Father Edmunds decided not to arrest

Ethelred, but he has actually entered his name as a student of the college."

"Oh, there's a joke somewhere!" cried Haines.

"That's what I said to Father Howard when he told me that Ethelred was admitted, but he laughed more than ever and told me that he wanted you all to keep together till he had presented you to Ethelred."

"We're not ready to meet him yet, Earl," said Ed Devereux. "There's not a rotten egg in the crowd."

"It's queer," commented Earl. "But we little fellows know that the president sees further than we, and—"

"Here comes Father Howard," broke in Devereux.

All turned quickly toward the entrance to the residence building. There at the top of the steps stood Father Howard, and holding the Father's hand in his own, a very small boy with a very pale face.

"Boys," said Father Howard, and, as he spoke, the crowd surged about the steps. "I want to introduce you to your new schoolmate, Ethelred Preston."

When the newcomer took off his sailor cap and, exposing a sunny head of ringlets, bowed gravely, he was facing such a staring, stupid, wondering, open-mouthed crowd of petrified figures as one seldom comes on in this world of constant surprises.

He was a singularly pretty boy, with very dark blue eyes and fair, regular features. In dress, he was a model of neatness. His every movement spoke refinement.

Earl was the first to recover himself. Running up the steps, he took the newcomer's hands.

"Are you really Ethelred Preston?"

"That is my name, sir," answered the lad with a smile and a bow.

"Three cheers for Mama's Darling!" cried Peter Lane, the small boy with the big voice.

Hats and caps went flying on high, while cheer upon cheer rent the air till little Ethelred was blushing like a rose.

Father Howard meanwhile was whispering in Earl's ear. Earl's face lighted up; he nodded assent and made a motion for silence.

"Ethelred Preston, you've got a nickname. It's Mama's Darling. How do you like that nickname?"

"I don't like it at all, if you please. I don't like nicknames."

"Very good; now I'll tell you what we boys will do. If you explain to us how you happen to be Ethelred Preston, and how it comes that the other Ethelred Preston is not you, we boys will agree to drop your nickname. Isn't that so, boys?"

There was a hearty and unanimous assent.

"Thank you, sir," said Ethelred. "I shall tell my story with pleasure, if Father Howard has no objections."

"It will be a pleasure for me to hear it from your lips, Ethelred."

"Thank you, Father."

And Ethelred began his story, and held his audience breathless for ten minutes.

There were certain circumstances, however, which he did not explain, but which came to light afterwards. These points, pieced into his narrative, will be set down in the following chapters.

Chapter XX

WHY ETHELRED FAILED TO REACH HENRYTON IN DUE TIME

IT was a chilly morning, late in January, when a closed carriage drove up to the station at Brighton. The coachman threw open the door, and there stepped out a lady and a little boy. The lady, evidently a woman of refinement, was in tasteful but modest attire; the boy's costume, on the other hand, was picturesque and much out of the ordinary. Any little girl would have detected in the ripple and splendor of his golden, ambrosial curls the constraining influence of the crimping irons. There were shining buckles upon his low shoes, the largeness of the buckles forcing into notice the smallness of his feet, and sober, black silk ribbons, tied in a bow-knot, bound his shapely knickerbockers at the knees. He wanted but a sash to complete his resemblance to that darling of all mothers and most girls—Little Lord Fauntleroy.

The woman was somewhat flushed about the eyes and had evidently been weeping. The boy, with compressed lips and frowning brow, held his face toward the ground. He was clearly in a pet.

From time to time she gazed at him with that pathetic look in which a mother's love unrequited so often expresses itself—but the boy gave her no heed. Involuntarily, a sigh broke from her.

The little fellow's face, despite himself, softened. He looked up and saw the love shining in that other face.

"Mama!" he cried, "*please* take me along with you."

"No, Ethelred dear," the mother made answer, as they walked into the deserted ladies' waiting-room; "your delicate constitution could not endure the hardships of a trip across the ocean at this rude season of the year. And indeed I am sorry that you may not come. You know, my darling, that I shall miss you far more than you will miss me. Try, dear, to be brave and cheerful." The mother's voice faltered on these words. She gathered herself together and added, "Make the parting easy for your mother, my only child."

And the kind, tender woman turned away her head and hid her face in her handkerchief. Let all of us who see by faith, as it were, and from afar the sacred and heroic love which mothers have for their little ones— let us, too, turn away our eyes and bow our heads before this loveliness of grief.

A moment passed in silence. Then Ethelred returned to the attack.

"But I don't want to go to a boarding school, Ma; the boys are so rough, and besides, at Henryton they are all Catholics."

"Yes, but there are many good Catholics,

Ethelred dear. I have known several myself. And Henryton College is so very well conducted. I met one of their boys last summer when I visited the sister of Mrs. Meriwether, her boy Earl. He was such a finished little gentleman that I felt anxious for you two to meet. And now I am forced to send you to the college where he is attending; and I feel sure, dear, that if you only put on a brave face, you will like the school very much."

"But, Mama!" cried Ethelred, putting his arm about his mother, "I can't bear to leave you."

Forgetting the time and place, Mrs. Preston threw her arms about the child's neck, and mother and son indulged in a "good cry."

Ethelred was the first to recover himself, and when he had wiped his eyes, the pout was done.

"Well, Mama, I'll go to please you."

"You darling!" cried the delighted mother, and she fell to gazing upon the pretty, somewhat effeminate features of her boy, as though for the last time. There was a slight lump in Ethelred's throat; and to relieve it, he gave a little hem.

"Have you your cough drops, dear?"

"Yes, Mama."

"Take one at once; the early morning air

is sharp, and your cold is not quite done. I put a bottle of cough medicine in your trunk; be sure and take it regularly, my darling. Oh, dear! How time flies—only five minutes more, and we shall be parted. Promise me, dear, not to put your head out of the car windows."

"I won't, Ma."

"And don't stand on the platform, Ethelred, and be sure to keep your seat. You will reach Henryton at nine o'clock this morning. Go direct to the College, dear; and don't spend your money on cakes and candies on the way, or you will make yourself sick."

Mrs. Preston went on with a series of "Don'ts" which lasted till the train which was to bear Ethelred away pulled up at the depot. I am sorry to say that Ethelred, who was something of a spoiled boy, took these prohibitions in bad part. He lapsed again into his pout and behaved, at a moment when signs of extreme affection are most expected, as spoiled children often do in such circumstances.

The fond mother, fearing that Ethelred might neglect some of her many injunctions, secured the ear of the conductor.

"Please keep your eye on my little boy, sir."

Ethelred bridled.

"See that he stays in the sleeper," continued Mrs. Preston. "Don't let him run around, please; and keep him out of danger, and—"

"Yes, ma'am—all aboard!"

The conductor waved his hand. Mrs. Preston snatched a last kiss and presently stood weeping and alone while the train moved away.

Ethelred, as he entered the sleeping-car, was in a bad mood. To have a conductor watching over him, as though he were a baby! If he had been an infant, his mother could hardly have varied her requests. Ethelred was something of a "baby" in the small boy's sense of the word, and being a baby, he resented his mother's course far more than a manlier boy would have resented it. To make matters worse, the conductor carried out Mrs. Preston's injunctions with a literalness that was most galling to the spoiled child. He repeated Mrs. Preston's words to the colored porter and added a few directions of his own within range of the small boy's burning ears. Ethelred was at one and the same time furious and frightened. Fifteen minutes had passed over these unpleasant emotions, when the train stopped at the station of a very pretty, little village.

Ethelred rose, and had gone as far as the platform, when he was stopped upon the steps by the porter.

"No you don't, Johnnie," he said jocosely. "Get right back into that car. You just keep quiet, and in an hour you'll be at Henryton."

"You think I'm a baby?" protested Ethelred.

"You were once, and you haven't got over it altogether."

A few loafers and a passenger laughed at this sally, and covered with shame, Ethelred retired into the sleeper.

He had hardly taken his seat when an overgrown boy with a big tray entered the car, looked about eagerly and finally fixed his small eyes upon Ethelred. After a short survey, he approached.

"I say, young feller," he said, seating himself beside the little lad, "I'd like to show you something that you want." As he spoke, he uncovered his tray and exposed to view a collection of cuffs, collars and odds and ends.

"See there! Look at these suspenders! I've got 'em all sizes, and for every age. Here's a pair will fit you. Just look at them galluses."

And with considerable enthusiasm shining from his eyes, the strange boy dangled a tiny pair of suspenders in Ethelred's face.

"If you please," said Ethelred, "I don't want any suspenders."

"But just feel 'em. See the way they stretch! They're just running over with elastic, and they'll last you till you're so big that you won't want to wear 'em anymore."

"I tell you I don't want them."

"You only think you don't want 'em. Why, I'll let you have this pair for sixty cents— they cost me seventy-five cents wholesale. I can swear to it."

"I tell you, I don't want them. I don't wear suspenders; I wear a belt."

The peddler gazed at Ethelred with much pity upon his mottled face.

"What! A feller your size not wearing suspenders! You ought to, unless you want to be a baby. Every boy that goes to school wears suspenders. Don't you go to school?"

"I'm on my way to school now, but I don't want to go to school."

"Then take a pair of suspenders with you. Here, I'll just give 'em to you. Take 'em for forty-five cents."

"If I want suspenders, I can get them at that old school."

"What school you going to?"

"Henryton College. I've been going to school all my life," continued Ethelred with a pout;

"at least, I've been kept at my books day after day, and I'm about tired of it; and besides I don't care about going to an old boarding college."

"I wish I had your chance," said the peddler. "Here I am seventeen years old and scarcely no schoolin'. I've been a peddlin' suspenders and things all my life pretty near, and I'm tired of it."

"I'd much rather peddle suspenders than go to school." Ethelred, as he spoke, pouted so successfully that he presented what is popularly known as a "baby face" to his new acquaintance. But that young man's sense of humor was not disturbed in the least.

"And I'd a heap rather go to school than peddle suspenders."

"A boarding school is a penitentiary," added Ethelred, with another baby face of disgust.

"You get clothed and lodged and eddicated, though. They learn you all kinds of things."

"But I don't want to learn. My head is tired of names of flowers and stars and all sorts of stuff. What I want is a holiday."

"Take these here for thirty-five cents?"

"No; I don't want suspenders."

The peddler made a feint of putting them away. He paused in the act, and said:

"Here, twenty-five cents."

Ethelred took the suspenders.

The peddler then put aside his box and, having carefully examined the silver quarter of a dollar, turned to Ethelred.

"My name is Packy Jarboe."

"Is that so?"

"Yes; people call me Packy, though my right name is Oliver. What's yourn?"

"Ethelred Preston."

"Was you ever at a boarding school before?"

"No."

"I never was myself."

"And I don't want to go. I'd rather dig potatoes or hold a plough."

"You said a while ago that you'd rather sell suspenders. Is that so?"

"Yes, indeed; I'd rather do anything."

Packy fell into a study.

"I'll tell you what, Preston. You'd like to sell suspenders, and I'd like to see what a boarding school is like. Suppose we change places."

"Oh, no."

"So you didn't mean what you said then? You were telling lies. You were just a-blowing."

"No, I wasn't. But we can't change places without being found out. Besides, even if I didn't care about going to boarding school, it doesn't follow that I feel like running away."

"Didn't you say jest a minute ago that you was never at a boarding school in your life?"

"Yes."

"Then the people who teach at that school don't know you—do they?"

"No; I never met any of them, and what is more, I don't want to meet any of them, either."

"And do you know any of the boys that go to that school?"

"No; I heard of one boy, Earl Meriwether. But I never saw one of them yet."

"Well, then, why couldn't I go on in your place. No one would know the difference."

Little Ethelred had not the courage to say that such an exchange would be wrong. Like most "mamas' darlings" he was weak. So he contented himself with answering:

"It would be all right, perhaps, for a day or two, but they would find out after a while that there was something wrong. You couldn't use my clothes, and when you'd open my trunk, everybody would see that the things in it could not possibly belong to you."

Packy Jarboe here made a digression, inquiring into the price of Ethelred's shoes and of various other articles. He offered incidentally to buy Ethelred a much "nattier suit" for five dollars. Ethelred did not happen to need a suit. Packy thereupon returned to the main question.

"You said just now that I could take your place for a day or so only without getting found out."

"Yes, and I'm sure it is so."

"Well, suppose we exchange places for two days?"

Ethelred looked alarmed.

"You needn't try to back out," continued Packy eagerly. "Here's the way we can do it. I'll go on right now to Henryton College and present myself as you. Today is Thursday, and I stay there today, and tomorrow night I clear out and you come in on Saturday morning."

"I'd rather not," said Ethelred, uneasily.

"But look! You'll have a fine show to learn what a peddler's life is. It will be lots of fun for you, and I'll have a chance to see how a boarding school is worked. I'll let you have my peddler's outfit, and I'll give you a map of my route. Just think of it—you'll be your own boss for two days."

Ethelred could not refrain from showing some pleasure at this last inducement.

"And then," continued the enterprising Packy, "it will be such a joke. You come to college on Saturday morning, and when the boys learn how you've fooled 'em, they'll think you're awful smart. It will be a great joke."

"That's so; but then I don't think I should like to—"

"Oh, well, if you're afraid to stand by what you've said, all right. You're a little coward and won't go anywhere without your mama's along. Them things on your knickerbockers at the knees are her apron strings, and you're tied to 'em."

"I'm not a coward, and I'm not afraid!" answered Ethelred, with flashing eyes, "only I don't care about trying that plan."

"You *are* a coward, and you *are* afraid, and I just *dare* you change places with me for two days. Ah, you little coward, you dasn't!"

"Just to show you that I'm not afraid," cried Ethelred, "I will change places with you! There! You think I can't take care of myself because I'm small! You may go to Henryton in my place, and now tell me what I'm to do."

"Shake hands on that," said Packy. "That's right. You've got more sand than I thought. Well, first of all, instead of getting off at Henryton, you get off at Collinsville, which isn't so far up the road—that's as far as my ticket goes. This morning and this afternoon you take in Collinsville and sell all the suspenders and notions you can there. Then this afternoon, about four, you start off for Hagartown, which is just seven miles from Collinsville."

"How do I get there?"

"It's not on the railroad; you walk."

"Walk seven miles!" cried Ethelred, opening his eyes and holding up his hands.

"Yes, of course. You're not a baby. There's no way of riding there. The railroad doesn't run through it, and you don't want to hire a kerridge. You must look out not to get lost; I'll tell you the way after a while, and if you forget it, you can ask most any person in Collinsville. It isn't seven miles," continued Packy, noticing Ethelred was still frightened; "it's only about four. I said seven to scare you. When you get to Hagartown, there's a sort of hotel the first thing you come to as you walk along the road. It's kept by an uncle of mine; and he'll give you a bed and supper and breakfast the next morning cheap. Then you go round and sell what you can in the village and stay that night at my uncle's again. Next morning, you leave the suspenders that are left over and the other traps with my uncle and all the money you've got in on the sales, and go back to Collinsville so as to catch the train that passes at eight-fifty for Henryton. See?"

"Yes, but I don't know how to sell all these things."

"I'll give you the prices on a list—it's all written out. And now you must show me how to play my part."

"They'll suspect something when you get to the college because they know I'm a little fellow."

"How do they know that?"

"Because Ma showed me the letter she wrote to the president of the college. She talks about her little Ethelred and tells him what care he must take of me. When the president sees you, he'll know there's something wrong."

"Don't you see any way of my getting over that?" asked Packy, anxiously.

"Why, yes," answered Ethelred, after a short pause and with some reluctance. "You know mothers don't notice how fast their children grow; you look as though you've been growing lately."

"That's so! I think I can talk them over on that."

"But why do you want to go to school for two days? There's no sense in that."

"Yes, there is. I want to get an idea of what it is like."

Packy counted on finding his profit out of the two days at Henryton. At the very worst, he could borrow five or six dollars. In any event, he trusted to his luck; he would contrive to be none the poorer for his two days away from his regular calling.

The two then fell to comparing notes. Ethelred told Packy about his mother, his home, Earl Meriwether, and crammed the enterprising peddler for his new role. He gave him a few of his visiting cards and provided him with the letter of recommendation from the pastor of his native town.

In return, Packy Jarboe furnished Ethelred with a price list, explaining very carefully, as he did so, all details. He also wrote out a little map showing the roads to be taken from Collinsville to Hagartown.

"There now," said Packy, passing over his stock to Ethelred, "you know your part and I know mine. Here we are at Collinsville—it's only twelve or thirteen miles from Henryton. Well, so long."

Packy helped Ethelred out and, once they were upon the platform of the station, showed himself very solicitous in adjusting about Ethelred's neck the strap which supported the pack. He hung over Ethelred for rather a long time, tugging here, pulling there.

Two hours later in the day, Ethelred missed three silver dollars from his vest-pocket and wondered how he could have lost them.

At the present moment, however, he stood very much confused and perplexed, watching the receding train and wondering how he had been so foolish and so wicked as to have allowed himself to be drawn into this cheap and dishonest trick.

"I'm a goose," he said to himself.

Poor Ethelred was right in his self-condemnation. Strictly speaking he was not a goose, but he had allowed a fit of peevishness and a bit of human respect to drag him into a position which was neither wise nor honorable.

The little lad, clad in a dainty suit and carrying a peddler's pack, excited no little interest and comment in the village of Collinsville. He had the polite ways of a home-bred boy, and people were astonished at the incongruity. Ladies who, as a rule, made short work of peddlers, were pleased to examine Ethelred's wares, and several of them made purchases. Ethelred began to enjoy the situation.

Before noon he had sold three dollars' worth of his goods. By this time the village youth had discovered him. They rallied

together, twelve or fifteen, and, in the simplicity of their heavy coats, coarse caps and
woolen mittens, began to pass invidious
remarks upon Ethelred's more complex
attire.

"We've just come out of a bandbox," said
one.

"Jest look at the latest style."

"Say, are you a boy or a girl?" inquired a
third.

Ethelred flushed.

"Go away, please," he said.

"There's a fellow here your size would like
to lick you," suggested another pleasantly,
and he put his hand upon a sturdy, tanned
lad no taller than Ethelred but much stouter.

"I'll do it with one hand tied behind my
back!" asserted this young bantam.

"Here you, Tommy Taggart, go home now,
or I'll tell your mother on you. Go away from
here, all you boys. Do you hear?"

The woman who thus interrupted the opening of hostilities was standing on the threshold of her house. Judging by her face and
manner, she was of more than ordinary consequence in Collinsville.

Tommy was the first to take his leave,
and the others, not slow to follow, left
Ethelred facing Mrs. Rainey.

"Thank you, ma'am," said Ethelred, removing his hat.

"What are you doing here, little boy?" continued Mrs. Rainey.

"I'm trying to sell all sorts of things, ma'am; I'm a peddler."

The lady cast a longing look upon the bright face before her and sighed. She had no child to gladden her home.

"It's a pity to see a little fellow like you at such work. You ought to be at school, my dear."

"I have been to school, ma'am, a good deal."

"I thought so; your manners are not what one would expect of a person of your calling. Where did you go to school?"

"Please, mayn't I show you some of my wares?" Ethelred, in thus changing the subject, evinced that he did not wish to enter into the question of his past life.

"Yes, child, come inside; it is cold. Don't you feel the weather?"

"My toes do, ma'am," returned the lad. "Thank you, I shall come in gladly."

Mrs. Rainey, who was the wife of the village banker, made several purchases.

"And now, my boy, won't you take dinner with me? I never asked a peddler to dinner before, but you are a little boy, a good little boy, and I can see behind it all a dear, loving mother."

Here Ethelred, as he thought of his mother, of his ungrateful parting from her, of his wayward conduct, could contain his emotions no longer and burst into a fit of weeping.

"There, there, my dear," said Mrs. Rainey, leaving the doorway, advancing to the gate and patting the boy on the head, "I see there is something sad in your past life and I won't ask you anything about it."

"Thank you, ma'am," said Ethelred. "There is something sad, but not the way you think. I am obliged to you for not asking me to explain. But I shall explain to you by letter in a few days. I am ashamed to, now."

Had Ethelred then and there unbosomed himself, as he felt prompted to do, he would have been spared much suffering; but shame held him silent. Even had he then and there resolved to bring to an end at once his career as a peddler, all might have gone well with him; but he had promised to do Packy's work faithfully, and he clung to his resolution.

Accordingly, after a hearty dinner and a pleasant chat with Mrs. Rainey, Ethelred, with profuse and sincere thanks, took up his pack and bade her farewell.

"So you are going to Hagartown, my dear?

You know the way, I suppose?"

"I've got a map of the roads which I am to take in my pocket, ma'am. This road past your house is the main road, isn't it?"

"Yes, my dear; you go along it for full two miles and a half before you turn. Good-bye."

The kind lady, in motherly fashion, kissed the little lad and said:

"Don't forget to write to me and to tell me your name and all about yourself. You have given me a very bright hour. God has showered his benefits upon me—a good husband, true friends, education, means; but, my dear, the little boy of mine, who should be about your age, lies over there."

And she pointed over toward the grave-yard, which she did not see, for her eyes were dimmed with tears. Ethelred departed thinking of his fond mother. Oh, how he wished he could recall that hour of parting and that silly conspiracy on board the train.

Ethelred was resolved henceforth to be a different boy in his dealings with his mother.

Half an hour's walk told upon him. He had been upon his feet for several hours of the morning, and the pack was heavy. More-over, he was unaccustomed to this manner of life. Worst of all, it was growing colder and the wind from the north made every step a struggle. He was a very tired, a very sad and a very repentant boy before he came to the first turn in the road.

And now the question was—which direction to take.

He laid down his pack and felt in his pockets for the rude map. It was gone! Then little Ethelred cried heartily, after the fashion of mamas' darlings in such circumstances. His feet were aching with the cold; his hands were benumbed. There was a strange feeling about his ears, not a sharp, but a dull, dead pain. He looked about him. There was not a house in sight, and to crown all, darkness was coming on apace over the dull, dead fields and the naked trees, through the branches of which the bitter wind howled in desolation.

It was getting colder every moment, and, inexperienced as he was, Ethelred recognized the danger of resting in such an exposure. He arose with a heavy heart and, trusting to luck, turned to the right.

And very soon (so weary and footsore had he become), he abandoned all hope of reaching Hagartown that night. In the distance, he saw a light shining. It was probably a farmhouse.

If he could only reach that light! On he trudged with failing step. The dull pains from the cold had grown duller; this cheered him.

Had he but known what this change meant, he would have been frightened. The boy was in danger of freezing to death.

At length after one of the weariest, longest quarters of an hour in his life, he came opposite the light. It shone from a large homestead back some fifty feet from the roadside fence.

With little difficulty, Ethelred found the gate and was feeling for the latch, when a low growl brought his heart to his mouth and a large mastiff came bounding toward him.

Ethelred stood in great fear of dogs; many who are not mamas' darlings share the same dread.

He turned and ran back the way he had come—ran till his legs refused to do their duty. The run promised to be disastrous in its consequences. He felt as if he were about to faint. Even the cold ground seemed to invite him. He thought of his mother, but he did not cry. It was a time to act, and act quickly.

Unfastening the pack, he threw it upon the road, and summoning all his strength, he made on, determined to reach Mrs. Rainey's house, which stood at the outskirts of the village.

Thus relieved by the abandonment of Packy

Jarboe's pack, for a few minutes he advanced with new energy, and he congratulated himself that the pain had all gone. But how drowsy he was getting! He felt that he could sleep for twenty-four hours at a stretch. More than once he was on the point of throwing himself upon the wayside. But some blind instinct withheld him from indulging in a sleep which would, in all likelihood, have known no waking.

At length he reached the main road and turned, oh, so wearily, toward Mrs. Rainey's.

In the distance, he saw another light. It was near. It was moving. Nearer and nearer it came, while upon the still air, there fell the sound of falling hoofs and moving wheels.

"Help!" called Ethelred.

A lantern flashed out from the buggy and moved about rapidly till it rested upon Ethelred.

"Are you the boy that was at Mrs. Rainey's?"

"Yes, let me in; I want to sleep."

A gentleman jumped from the buggy, ran up to Ethelred, and as he threw the light upon his face and noticed how white the extremities had become, he exclaimed:

"My God! Just in time. The boy is freezing to death."

Ethelred did not hear this; he had fallen into the man's arms an inert mass. Quickly conveying him to the buggy, the man forced some liquor down his throat, wrapped him carefully in a large buffalo robe and, turning round, touched his horse with the whip.

The animal was a blooded horse. He sprang forward with all speed, as though he realized he were racing against death.

"Go on, Prince; go on!" cried the driver. "Go on, old boy, if it's your last race!"

In little more than four minutes they drew up at Mrs. Rainey's. Even as they paused, the good woman threw open the door.

"Did you find him?" she cried.

"Yes, wife, your presentiment was correct; I was just in time to catch the boy before he was frozen." As Mr. Rainey spoke, he came hurrying across the lawn with the boy bundled as he was in the robe.

"Here, my dear, take him in charge, while I go off again for Doctor Marmon; I shall be back in ten minutes."

It was an anxious hour that followed, but thanks to care and love and sacrifice and prompt medical treatment, the boy was soon pronounced out of danger.

In the evening paper of the following day, there was published this item of news:

ADVENTURES OF A PEDDLER
He Didn't Know the Way, and the
Day Was Cold

A very small boy undertook to be a peddler. Probably he will try some other occupation when he recovers. He started out bravely yesterday morning and did quite well, but found out before night that it was a cold day. In going afoot from Collinsville to Hagartown, the enterprizing youth lost his road and was nearly frozen to death. Mr. Rainey, one of the leading citizens of Collinsville, picked him up in an unconscious condition. A reporter tried to have an interview with the partially thawed-out young gentleman, but Mrs. Rainey objected, asserting that the boy was too sick to talk. His name and place of residence are still unknown. The youngster, who is described as a rather pretty lad, strangely dressed for one in his class of life, will not be able to get about for several days; and it is not likely that he will be quite so chipper when next he takes the road.

It was this bit of cheap newspaper wit which caused Packy Jarboe such surprise at the railroad station on the night of his first attempt at running away. On the instant he changed his plans. He would return to college and spend a few more days in the hope of fleecing some of the students. The danger of detection was great, but Packy did not mind taking a risk.

Before returning to the college, Packy scribbled a note to his uncle, the hotel-keeper, in which, without disclosing fully the state of affairs, he entreated him to send him a health bulletin every day concerning the boy who lay sick at Mr. Rainey's house. The answers were to be forwarded to Master Packy Jarboe, Henryton P. O.

Packy next made a confederate and mail carrier of the day scholar Farwell and thus succeeded in keeping informed of Ethelred's movements.

The following letter was the last which he received:

> Tuesday, Jan. 31st, 189–
> *Deer Nevew:* The boy is getting round quite smart and will leave Ranies next wensday. They say he is going to a skule. He is not a peddler. I seen him today. He was sittin' in a window and looked tollable. Why are you so anxous about his helth?
>
> Your lovin' uncle,
> Calvin Jarboe

Packy had anticipated the news contained in this note and was prepared when he received it to run away at an hour's notice. He took to flight, accordingly, after studies on the same evening, with what results the reader already knows.

Chapter XXI

IN WHICH ETHELRED FINDS THE BEST OF MOTHERS

"WELL, my dear," said Mrs. Rainey, on Thursday morning, "we shall have to lose you."

"No, it is I who am going to lose you, ma'am," said little Ethelred, who, seated at the breakfast table, was eating with the appetite which youth and convalescence are wont to develop. "Only for your kindness, I don't know what would have happened to me."

"I took your mother's place, dear," said Mrs. Rainey simply. "When you told me your story yesterday I was so relieved. So long as I did not know the true circumstances of the case, it pained me to think that you were to take up that wretched peddlers' life again."

"*That* is over," said Ethelred. "I've been taught a lesson. When Mama comes back I think she will find me a different boy. I felt awful sorry for my conduct toward her after I left you that day and began to freeze on the road. And then, ma'am, since I've been with you, I've learned a lot. One of the reasons I had for going off as a peddler was because Henryton College was a Catholic school. The people around our place are all bitter against Catholics, and I believed everything I heard."

"No one can blame you for that, Ethelred."

"You were the first Catholic I ever met, Mrs. Rainey, and when I came to myself in your house and saw a crucifix over the bed I was on, and a picture of the Virgin, I saw your kind face bending down over me too; and there were tears of joy in your eyes because I had come to myself. Then I felt that there couldn't be anything so bad about Catholics. And you were just like my mother the way you treated me."

Mrs. Rainey's face grew very tender as she listened.

"And sometimes," continued the eloquent lad, "when you thought I was asleep, I wasn't; and I used to watch you saying prayers on beads.

I liked to look at your face then; it used to look something like the beautiful face of the Virgin in the picture.

"No, I'm in earnest," pursued Ethelred, noticing Mrs. Rainey's deprecatory gesture. "And now I shall always be glad to see a crucifix or a picture of the Virgin, for they will make me remember your kindness."

Mrs. Rainey kissed the little boy, but said nothing.

"I'm ashamed to write to Mama about my conduct, Mrs. Rainey, and I hope you'll do it for me. I know you will put it kindly, and don't forget to tell her how sorry I am."

"I shall write to her this day, Ethelred, and will tell her that you are now well and about to go to college, and that you go there with a strong intention of doing well."

"Thank you, ma'am. In a day or so, when I get settled down at Henryton, I will write to her myself and tell her of your kindness; and I will tell her too that I intend wearing that Miraculous Medal you gave me around my neck till I die."

With regard to the Miraculous Medal, a word of explanation should be given. An hour or two after Ethelred's departure from her home, Mrs. Rainey, as was her custom, said some short prayers to the Blessed Virgin, concluding with a petition for the safety of the little peddler. She kissed her medal at the end and, even as she did so, it was borne in upon her that the boy peddler was in danger. Mrs. Rainey went over to the window and threw it open. It was a biting breeze that blew upon her. She had not thought it so cold.

How could a child such as he bear exposure to such a temperature?

Mrs. Rainey took out her beads and said them earnestly for the little wanderer, whose pretty ways and childlike innocence had won her heart. She was finishing the last decade when the sound of wheels without brought her breathless to the gate.

"Don't get out yet, James," she said to her husband. "There's a little boy peddler gone down the road to Hagartown, and I feel sure that he is in danger. He is no ordinary peddler, and there is something mysterious about him. He looks as if he could not stand much exposure. It may be imagination, but I shall not rest tonight unless I know that something has been done to help him. He was on his way to Jarboe's hotel. Won't you please—oh, but you must be cold. Here, let me go. It's a short drive."

"I'm not that kind of a man, Martha. Cold!

Why, I feel as comfortable as a polar bear. You may be mistaken, but, mistake or not, it's a charitable and a kind impulse. Get up there, Prince! I say, Martha," he added, as the horse turned, "have a warm supper ready, and good-bye."

And when Mr. Rainey returned with the poor boy, one of the first things Mrs. Rainey did was to put her Miraculous Medal on the breast of the sufferer and commission his recovery to the office of the Immaculate Queen.

All of this she had told Ethelred with her usual simplicity; and Ethelred, looking at her, had said:

"Mama is one, and you are two, and *she*"—holding up the medal—"is three. I have three mothers now."

Mrs. Rainey accompanied Ethelred to Henryton. She told her beautiful story to the president; and had she really been Ethelred's own mother, she could not have pleaded more effectually for the runaway. The boy was received unconditionally.

Chapter the Last

"WHAT a happy crowd!" exclaimed Father Noland as he entered the boy's refectory on the morning of the First Friday in February.

"Come here, Father!" "Come here!" "Sit near me!" "This is the best place!"

The eager, young voices produced a babel of welcome, while the good old Father stood smiling and undecided. Earl, the First Communicant, sat at the head of the table; and the loveliness of his soul seemed to shine forth from his noble face. To his right, scarcely less happy, sat little Ethelred, and to his left that giddy young Godfather, Eddie Devereux, who could not sit still for very joy but kept bobbing up and down like a jack-in-the-box. Roger Haines and Peter Lane were there too; and waiting upon the breakfast party were the vice president and the venerable treasurer of the college.

"It's all like a story out of a book, Father Noland!" cried Eddie Devereux, who had leaped up and, catching the Father's cincture, gently forced him to the place nearest Earl. "We thought we had a lot of adventures here, but the real Ethelred Preston's story beat ours."

"There was some sort of providence in the whole matter," said Earl gravely. "I couldn't help thinking of it this morning after Communion. Just one week ago, I was determined never to become a Catholic. I was angry and spiteful and I really thought that I should never change. And do you know, Ethelred, that if you had arrived that day as you should have arrived, I believe that I should have stuck to my resolution?"

Little Ethelred stopped eating to put on the look of astonishment.

"You see, you're a nice fellow and you have a good home training. There isn't a boy in the yard that is better off in that respect than you are. Most of us, in judging others, go a great deal by manners, and I'd have compared you with the average Catholic boys here, which would not have been to their advantage, and you would have helped to confirm me in my notion of sticking to Protestantism."

"You are going to be an analyst, Earl," said Father Noland. "What you say is quite true. Most of us judge by the exterior, and outward respectability is often taken for morality and religion."

"And, perhaps for that very reason, it was the false Ethelred that threw cold water on my resolution."

"So, then, the boy you call Mama's Darling converted you?" observed Ethelred.

"He certainly had a great deal to do with it."

"Which shows," put in Father Noland, "in what wondrous ways God brings about His holy Will."

"So Mama's Darling, by coming here, did a heap of good without knowing it," said Roger.

"And just think of all the fun he afforded us!" chimed in Devereux.

"In fact, he has done good to almost everyone except himself," said Earl. "What a pity he didn't get some improvement out of the adventure."

"Perhaps he has, my boy," said Father Noland. "The boy's dishonest schemes all went wrong—that may be a lesson. Again, he has been in good company for a week— and no one but God knows how much hidden good is done by good example. You yourself, Earl, were very kind to him; and I cannot think that all your kindness has gone for nothing. Let us hope that the boy may be better and wiser for his adventures and misadventures at Henryton College."

"I feel bound to pray for him; without intending it, he did me a great deal of good," said Earl.

"And you, Ethelred, what have you to say for yourself?" asked Father Noland.

"I can't say all I'd like and eat my breakfast, sir. These biscuits are better than our cook's. But it seems to me that if I had come to college the day I should have come, I'd have been chock-full of ugliness. I hated Catholics, and I was angry at Mama, and I wouldn't have studied. I did wrong by going off peddling, but God punished me. He nearly froze my ears off."

"When God is particularly good, He punishes us swiftly," observed Father Harter. "When the punishment comes tripping upon the heels of the fault, we see the connection and we repent."

"That's the way it was with me, sir. The night I was freezing, I prayed in earnest, and I think God heard me. And then it looks as if the Virgin helped to save me. And then I was treated so nicely at Mrs. Rainey's; it knocked the bottom out of all my prejudices."

"Talks like a book, doesn't he?" whispered Eddie to Roger.

"Well, Ethelred," said Earl, with his kind, winning smile, "there's more than that coming to you from your adventure."

"What else, Earl?"

"I'm thinking of that medal upon your breast. It is going to convert your Mama and you too, some of these days."

Ethelred turned his eyes down and blushed; Earl had touched the wish which Mrs. Rainey by her goodness had inspired and which the company now about him had strengthened. His mother, be it remembered, left him to choose his own religion.

And within a year, all who were present at the First Communion breakfast recalled the remark and wondered, in the light of its coming true, whether it had been a prediction or a prophecy.

THE END

If you have enjoyed this book, consider making your next selection from among the following . . .

Prices subject to change.

Prices subject to change.

Prices subject to change.

Prices subject to change.

Catholic Books for Young People

Catholic Children's Treasure Box Books 1-10 (Ages 3-8+) . . 50.00
Catholic Children's Treasure Box Books 11-20 (Ages 3-8+) . . 50.00
My Confession Book. *Sr. M. A. Welters*. (Ages 6-10) 2.00
My See and Pray Missal. *Sr. J. Therese*. (Ages 4-8) 2.00
Set of 20 Saints' Lives by Mary Fabyan Windeatt. 160.00
Children of Fatima. *Windeatt*. (Ages 10 & up) 11.00
Curé of Ars. *Windeatt*. (Ages 10 & up) 13.00
Little Flower. *Windeatt*. (Ages 10 & up) 11.00
Patron St./First Communicants. *Windeatt*. (Ages 10 & up) . . . 8.00
Miraculous Medal. *Windeatt*. (Ages 10 & up) 9.00
St. Thomas Aquinas. *Windeatt*. (Ages 10 & up) 8.00
St. Catherine of Siena. *Windeatt*. (Ages 10 & up) 7.00
St. Rose of Lima. *Windeatt*. (Ages 10 & up) 10.00
St. Benedict. *Windeatt*. (Ages 10 & up) 11.00
St. Louis De Montfort. *Windeatt*. (Ages 10 & up) 13.00
Saint Hyacinth of Poland. *Windeatt*. (Ages 10 & up) 13.00
Saint Martin de Porres. *Windeatt*. (Ages 10 & up) 10.00
Pauline Jaricot. *Windeatt*. (Ages 10 & up) 15.00
St. Paul the Apostle. *Windeatt*. (Ages 10 & up) 15.00
King David and His Songs. *Windeatt*. (Ages 10 & up) 11.00
St. Francis Solano. *Windeatt*. (Ages 10 & up) 14.00
St. John Masias. *Windeatt*. (Ages 10 & up) 11.00
Blessed Marie of New France. *Windeatt*. (Ages 10 & up) . . . 11.00
St. Margaret Mary. *Windeatt*. (Ages 10 & up) 14.00
St. Dominic. *Windeatt*. (Ages 10 & up) 11.00
Anne—Life/Ven. Anne de Guigne (1911-1922). *Benedictine Nun*. 7.00
Under Angel Wings—True Story/Young Girl & Guardian Angel. 9.00
Pope St. Pius X. *F. A. Forbes*. 11.00
Child's Bible History. *M. Rev. F. J. Knecht*. 7.00
Forty Dreams of St. John Bosco. *St. John Bosco* 15.00
Blessed Miguel Pro—20th Century Mexican Martyr. *Ann Ball* 7.50
Story of a Soul. *St. Therese*. 9.00
The Guardian Angels. 3.00
St. Maria Goretti—In Garments All Red. *Fr. G. Poage*. 7.00
The Curé of Ars—Patron Saint of Parish Priests. *Fr. O'Brien*. 7.50
St. Maximilian Kolbe—Knight of the Immaculata. *Fr. J. J. Smith*. 7.00
Life of Blessed Margaret of Castello. *Bonniwell*. 9.00
Story/Church—Her Founding/Mission/Progress. (7th-12th Grades) 22.50
Bible History. *Johnson, Hannan & Dominica*. (Grades 6-9+) . 24.00
Bible History Workbook (to accompany above). *Ignatz*. 21.00
Set: Bible History Text & Workbook. 36.00

Prices subject to change.

St. Teresa of Avila. *F. A. Forbes*. (Youth–Adult) 7.00
St. Ignatius Loyola. *F. A. Forbes*. (Youth–Adult) 7.00
St. Athanasius. *F. A. Forbes*. (Youth–Adult) 7.00
St. Vincent de Paul. *F. A. Forbes*. (Youth–Adult) 7.00
St. Catherine of Siena. *F. A. Forbes*. (Youth–Adult) 7.00
St. John Bosco—Friend of Youth. *F. A. Forbes*. (Youth–Adult) 9.00
St. Monica. *F. A. Forbes*. (Youth–Adult) 7.00
Set of 7 Saints' Lives above by F. A. Forbes. ($51.00 value) 39.00
Set of 24 Catholic Story Coloring Books. *Windeatt & Harmon* 72.00
Our Lady of Fatima Catholic Story Coloring Book. 4.50
Our Lady of Lourdes Catholic Story Coloring Book. 4.50
Our Lady of Guadalupe Catholic Story Coloring Book. . . . 4.50
Our Lady of the Miraculous Medal Catholic Story Coloring Bk. 4.50
Our Lady of La Salette Catholic Story Coloring Book. 4.50
Our Lady of Knock Catholic Story Coloring Book. 4.50
Our Lady of Beauraing Catholic Story Coloring Book. 4.50
Our Lady of Banneux Catholic Story Coloring Book. 4.50
Our Lady of Pontmain Catholic Story Coloring Book. 4.50
Our Lady of Pellevoisin Catholic Story Coloring Book. . . . 4.50
St. Joan of Arc Catholic Story Coloring Book. 4.50
St. Francis of Assisi Catholic Story Coloring Book. 4.50
St. Anthony of Padua Catholic Story Coloring Book. 4.50
St. Dominic Savio Catholic Story Coloring Book. 4.50
St. Pius X Catholic Story Coloring Book. 4.50
St. Teresa of Avila Catholic Story Coloring Book. 4.50
St. Philomena Catholic Story Coloring Book. 4.50
St. Maria Goretti Catholic Story Coloring Book. 4.50
St. Frances Cabrini Catholic Story Coloring Book. 4.50
St. Christopher Catholic Story Coloring Book. 4.50
St. Meinrad Catholic Story Coloring Book. 4.50
Bl. Kateri Tekakwitha Catholic Story Coloring Book. 4.50
The Rosary Catholic Story Coloring Book. 4.50
The Brown Scapular Catholic Story Coloring Book. 4.50
Christ the King—Lord of History. *Anne Carroll*. (H. S. Text). 24.00
Christ the King, Lord of History Workbook. *Mooney*.. . . . . . 21.00
Set: Christ the King Text and Workbook. 36.00
Christ and the Americas. *Anne Carroll*. (High School Text). . 24.00
Old World and America. *Bishop Furlong*. (Grades 5-8). . . . 21.00
Old World and America Answer Key. *McDevitt*. 10.00
Our Pioneers and Patriots. *Bishop Furlong*. (Grades 5-8). . . . 24.00
Our Pioneers and Patriots Answer Key. *McDevitt*. (Grades 5-8). 10.00

At your Bookdealer or direct from the Publisher.
Toll Free 1-800-437-5876　　　　***www.tanbooks.com***

Prices subject to change.

From the cover of Tom Playfair . . .

TOM PLAYFAIR is one of "Fr. Finn's Famous Three"—**Tom Playfair**, **Percy Wynn** and **Harry Dee**. These were the most popular of Fr. Finn's 27 Catholic novels for young people. Resembling a Catholic version of Charles Dickens' stories, or even *The Hardy Boys*, these books were read by hundreds of thousands of young people in the late 19th and early-to-mid 20th century. Their quaint turn-of-the-century language is part of the charm of the stories and of Fr. Finn's own brand of humor. After young readers (or hearers) have "gotten into" his style, they find it hilarious! But besides being fun, the stories have a moral: Tom Playfair is an unruly little boy when he is sent to St. Maure's boarding school, but he develops into a good Catholic young man and leader—without ever losing his high spirits. (All 3 books feature Tom Playfair.)

But what about today's young people?

We were given great encouragement to reprint these books by the experience of a teaching Sister who reads all 3 books each year to her 5th and 6th graders—with very gratifying results. Sister says she has seen drastic changes in students after hearing Fr. Finn's stories—marked improvement in behavior, motivation *and character*, especially in boys. Though both boys and girls enjoy the books immensely, she says, "It's the boys that absolutely love them. It's a hero worship thing." And parents ask: "Who's this Tom Playfair?—because that's all the kids talk about at the dinner table on Monday nights."

Grade level: 5th-8th (and older!)

Tom Playfair
was "the most successful
book for Catholic boys and girls
ever published in the English
language." —Benziger
Brothers Publishers

Perfect for reading
aloud at home or at
school! Great for book
reports! Include an
"About the Author."

TOM PLAYFAIR

The story opens with 10-year-old Tom Playfair being quite a handful for his well-meaning but soft-hearted aunt. (Tom's mother has died.) Mr. Playfair decides to ship his son off to St. Maure's boarding school—an all-boys academy run by Jesuits—to shape him up, as well as to help him make a good preparation for his upcoming First Communion. Tom's adventures are just about to begin. Life at St. Maure's will not be dull!

PERCY WYNN

In this volume, Tom Playfair meets a new boy just arriving at St. Maure's. Percy Wynn has grown up in a family of 10 girls and only 1 boy—himself! His manners are formal, he talks like a book, and he has never played baseball or gone skating, boating, fishing, or even swimming! Yet he has brains, courage and high Catholic ideals. Tom and his buddies at St. Maure's befriend Percy and have a great time as they all work at turning Percy into an all-American Catholic boy.

HARRY DEE

Young Harry Dee arrives at St. Maure's thin and pale from his painful experiences involving the murder of his rich uncle. In this last book of the three, Tom and Percy help Harry recover from his early trauma—which involves solving "the mystery of Tower Hill Mansion." After many wild experiences, the three boys graduate from St. Maure's and head toward the life work to which God is calling each of them as young men.

THE TOM PLAYFAIR SERIES
By Fr. Francis J. Finn, S.J.

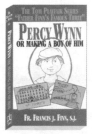

❶

❷

❸

These 3 books are the most popular of Fr. Finn's 27 Catholic novels for young people. Resembling a Catholic version of *Tom Sawyer*, these books have been read by hundreds of thousands of young people. Their quaint turn-of-the-century language is part of the charm of the stories and of Fr. Finn's own brand of humor. After young readers (or hearers) have "gotten into" his style, they find it hilarious!

But besides being fun, the stories have a moral: Tom is an unruly little boy when he is sent to St. Maure's boarding school, but after many adventures he and his friends develop into good Catholic young men and leaders—without ever losing their high spirits. (All three books feature Tom Playfair.) Young Catholics today love the Playfair books too!

Fr. Francis J. Finn, S.J. with *Dial* staff at St. Mary's College, St. Mary's, Kansas, 1894-1895.

ABOUT THE AUTHOR

Fr. Francis J. Finn, S.J.
1859-1928

T HE son of Irish immigrant parents, Francis J. Finn, S.J. was born on October 4, 1859 in St. Louis, Missouri; there he grew up, attending parochial schools. As a boy, Francis was deeply impressed with Cardinal Wiseman's famous novel of the early Christian martyrs, *Fabiola*. After that, religion really began to mean something to him.

Eleven-year-old Francis was a voracious reader; he read the works of Charles Dickens, devouring *Nicholas Nickleby* and *The Pickwick Papers*. From his First Communion at age 12, Francis began to desire to become a Jesuit priest; but then his fervor cooled, his grades dropped, and his vocation might have been lost except for Fr. Charles Coppens. Fr. Coppens urged Francis to apply himself to his Latin, to improve it by using an all-Latin prayerbook, and to read good Catholic books. Fr. Finn credited the saving of his vocation to this advice and to his membership in the Sodality of Our Lady.

Francis began his Jesuit novitiate and seminary studies on March 24, 1879. As a young Jesuit scholastic, he suffered from repeated bouts of sickness. He would be sent home to recover, would return in robust health, then would come down with another ailment. Normally this would have been seen as a sign that he did not have a vocation, yet his superiors kept him on. Fr. Finn commented, "God often uses instruments most unfit to do His work."

During his seminary days Mr. Finn was assigned as prefect of St. Mary's boarding school or "college" in St. Mary's, Kansas (which became the fictional "St. Maure's"). There he learned—often the hard way—how to teach and discipline boys.

ABOUT THE AUTHOR

One afternoon while supervising a class who were busy writing a composition, Mr. Finn thought of how they represented to him the typical American Catholic boy. With nothing else to do, he took up pencil and paper. "Why not write about such boys as are before me?" he asked himself. In no time at all he had dashed off the first chapter of *Tom Playfair*. When he read it aloud to the class, they loved it! Of course they wanted more.

Francis was finally ordained to the priesthood around 1891. This was the year that *Tom Playfair* was published. Fr. Finn's publisher, Benziger Brothers, was to call *Tom Playfair* "the most successful book for boys and girls ever published in the English language." Fr. Finn would write 27 books in all, which would be translated into as many as ten languages, and even into Braille.

Fr. Finn spent many years of his priestly life at St. Xavier's in Cincinati. There he was well loved, and it is said that wherever he went—if he took a taxi, ate at a restaurant, attended a baseball game—people would not take his money for their services, but instead would press money into his hand for his many charities. Children especially loved him. It is said that at his death in 1928, children by the thousands turned out to mourn their departed friend.

It was Fr. Finn's lifelong conviction that "One of the greatest things in the world is to get the right book into the hands of the right boy or girl. No one can indulge in reading to any extent without being largely influenced for better or worse."

According to the *American Catholic Who's Who*, Fr. Finn is "universally acknowledged the foremost Catholic writer of fiction for young people."

Photo of Fr. Finn courtesy of Midwest Jesuit Archives, St. Louis, Missouri. Biographical sketch from various sources, including an article in *Crusade* magazine which was based on Fr. Finn's memoirs as edited and published by Fr. Daniel A. Lord, S.J., in a book entitled *Fr. Finn, S.J.*